Gossamer Stories
and
Smoke-colored Stories

Gossamer Stories
and
Smoke-colored Stories

(Cuentos frágiles y Cuentos color de humo)

Manuel Gutiérrez Nájera

Gossamer Stories and
Smoke-colored Stories

SOJOURNER BOOKS

https://sojournerbooks.com

Translated by Daniel Bernardo from

Cuentos frágiles y Cuentos color de humo

ISBN: 978-1-989586-08-2

Table of Contents

SMOKE-COLORED STORIES

Preface

Manuel Gutiérrez Nájera (1859-1895) was a writer, poet, journalist and political figure.

He was born and lived in Mexico City.

In his writings he blended romanticism, modernism and symbolism. He wrote under different pseudonyms alongside his writing career, which he begun at the age of thirteen.

Together with Carlos Díaz Dufóo, he founded *Revista Azul*, which was the diffuser of Modernism in Mexico.

He wrote poetry and many short stories as well; the book of stories *Cuentos frágiles* (Gossamer Stories) was the only one that he published in life (1883).

Most of his work was published in different newspapers and magazines. Due to his premature death as well as his willingness to use a wide range of pen names, most of Gutiérrez Nájera's works were arranged into collections posthumously. He ordered with different criteria his writings for different newspapers and magazines: *Sunday Stories, Smoke-colored Stories, Gold-colored Stories, Rain-colored Stories*, etc. This has helped his editors to collect his histories in different books..

Manuel Gutiérrez Nájera is defined as a "kind of smile of the soul" by his graceful style, elegant, delicate and with tenderness of feelings.

His short stories show a world with plenty of suffering, but also irony and mockery.

This book contains his *Cuentos frágiles* (Gossamer Stories), with eighteen stories and *Cuentos color de humo* (Smoke-colored Stories), consisting of nine stories.

Gossamer Stories

New Year's ballad

In the quilted, silent, padded alcove, the patient's soft breath is barely heard. The curtains are stretched out; the candle spreads around its discreet light, and the blessed image of the Virgin candles at the head of the bed. Baby is bad, very bad... Baby dies...

The Doctor has auscultated the white chest of the sick child; with his thick hands he takes the tiny hands of the poor angel, and frowning, he looks sadly at the child and his parents. He asks for a piece of paper; he approaches the bedside table, and with his golden pen he writes... he writes. You only hear in the bedroom, like the heavy fluttering of a fly, the noise of the pen running over the paper, white and porous. The child sleeps; he has no strength to open his eyes. His face, once so flattering and rosy, is whiter and more transparent than wax: in his temples the bluish net of veins is outlined. His lips are pale, withered, skinned by disease. His little hands are as cold as two ice floes... Baby is bad... Baby is very bad... Baby is going to die...

Clara doesn't cry; she doesn't have tears anymore. And then, if she cried, she would wake up her poor child. What will the Doctor write? It's the prescription! Ah, if Clara knew, she would relieve him in an instant! For what, nothing can be done against evil? Is there no means to save an existence that is being extinguished? Ah! yes, there are, there must be; God is good, God does not want the torment of mothers; doctors are clumsy, they are unloving; they do not care much for the deep affliction of loving fathers:

that is why Baby is not yet relieved; that is why Baby is still very bad; that is why Baby, poor Baby, is going to die! And Clara says with tears in her eyes:

Ah! if only I knew!...

The unbearable calm of the Doctor irritates her. Why doesn't he save him? Why doesn't he give him back his health? Why doesn't he devote all his vigils, all his worries, all his studies? What, can't he? Then medicine is useless: it is a deception, it is a lie, it is an infamy. What have so many men done, so many wise men, if they do not know how to save this pain to the heart, if they cannot save the life of a child, of a being who has done no harm to anyone, who does not offend anyone, who is the smile, and is the light, and is the perfume of the house?

And the Doctor writes, writes, What medicine will he order? Will he again martyr his white flesh with those frightful instruments? –No, not anymore –says the mother–, I don't want that anymore. The son of my soul twists his arms, moves between those hard hands that squeeze him, turns his eyes blank, cries, cries a lot, begs, cries, until he can no longer continue, until the irresistible force of pain overcomes him, and he remains in his cradle still, senseless and still complaining, in a very low voice, about those knives, those pliers, those hooks that torment him, those heartless Doctors who appraise his body, and his mother, his poor mother who leaves him alone. No, I don't want those tortures anymore. They tie me up too, but they leave my ears free so that I can hear his tears, his complaints. I hear him, and I don't defend him! I see that they are killing him, and I consent to it!

The child sleeps, and the Doctor writes, writes. –My God, my God! Don't want him to die: send me another pain, another torment: I deserve it. But don't remove him from me, no, don't take it away. And Clare drowns her sobs, bites her handkerchief, wants to kiss him and embrace him –perhaps those last caresses– but the poor sick child is asleep, and his mother doesn't want him to wake up.

Clara sees him, sees him constantly with her big black and serene eyes, as if she fears that, when she stops looking at him, he will fly to heaven. How much havoc the disease has wrought on him! His chubby arms, today are thin, very thin. They no longer laugh in their elbows those two dimples so funny, that they kissed and caressed so many times. His eyes –black like his mother's– are enlarged by the dark circles under his eyes, by those pale violets of death. His blond hair forms him like the halo of a saint.

–My God, my God! I don't want him to die!

Baby is four years old. When he runs, it looks like he's going to fall. When he speaks, the words are pushed and run over his lips. He was very healthy: Baby had nothing: Pablo and Clara looked at each other in him and told each other at night about his mischief and his graces, without ever getting tired. But one afternoon Baby did not want to run through the garden; he felt cold: a sharp pain stuck in his temples, and he asked his mother to put him to bed. Baby went to bed that afternoon, and he's still not up. There they are, at the foot of the bed, and waiting for him, the little boots that still have the wet sand of the garden on the sole.

The Doctor has finished writing, but he won't leave. Well, what's so bad about him? The lackey runs to the apothecary.

–Doctor, Doctor! Is my child going to die?

The doctor answers in a very low voice:

–Calm down, don't let the boy wake up.

That's when Pablo arrives. Fifteen minutes ago, he left that bedroom, and it looks like a century to him. He came running like a madman. When he turned the corner he didn't want to raise his eyes, because he didn't want to see if the balcony was open. He looks at the Doctor's face and the mother's clasped hands; but he calms down: the blond angel is still sleeping in his crib –he's not gone!–. A minute later, the boy changes his posture, opens his eyes little by little and says with a voice barely audible:

Mom! Mom!...

–What do you want, my life? Aren't you better? Tell me what you feel! Poor me! Bring your little hands here, I'll warm them up! You'll be relieved, soul of my soul. I have commanded the Blessed Sacrament to light two candles. The Mother of Light is going to make you good.

The child turns his black eyes around, as if asking for shelter. Clara kisses him on the forehead, on the eyes, on the head, everywhere. Now she can kiss him! But in that effusion of love and tenderness, her eyes, once so dry, are full of tears, and Clara does not know if she kisses or cries. Some burning tears fall in the child's throat. The sick child, who has barely a voice to complain, says:

–Mom, Mom, don't cry!

Clara bites her handkerchief, the pillows, the crib mattress. Pablo approaches. It's time for him to kiss him too. It's his turn. He's strong, he's a man, he doesn't cry. And in the meantime, the Doctor, who has gone away, stirs the herbal tea with the little golden spoon. What is the wise man before death? The molecule of sand that will cover the ocean with its waves.

–Baby, baby, my life! Cheer up, get up. Today is the New Year. Come! Here in your little hand are the things that I went to buy you in the morning. The cone of sweets, for when you are better; the hoop with which you are going to run in the garden; the ball of colors for you to play in the yard. All that you have asked me!

Baby, the poor Baby, imprisoned in his cradle, dreamed of the open air, of the light of the sun, of the earth of the field and of the flowers ajar. That's why he just asked for those toys.

–If you're relieved, I'll buy you a wagon and two white sheep to drag it along... But cheer up, my angel, my life! Do you want a velocipede better?

Yes...? But if you fall? Give me your hands. Why are they cold? Does your head hurt a lot? Look, here's the big country house you asked for...

The eyes of the sick child light up. He gets up a little and hugs the big wooden box that his father brought him. He looks back at the table and looks sadly at the cone of sweets.

–Mom, Mom, I want a candy.

Clara, who is crying at the foot of the bed, consults the Doctor with her eyes; the Doctor consents, and Pablo, unhooking the cone, unties the ribbons and offers it to the child. Baby takes an almond with his little yellow fingers, and says:

–Dad, open your mouth.

Pablo, the man, the strong one, feels that he can't endure more; he kisses the fingers that put that almond between his lips, and he cries, he cries a lot.

Baby falls prostrate again. Her feet have become very cold; Clara squeezes them with her hands and kisses them. All useless! The Doctor prepares a tightly closed vessel filled with almost boiling water. He puts it on the sick child's feet. He doesn't speak anymore, he doesn't look anymore, he doesn't complain anymore; he just coughs, and from time to time he says in a barely perceptible voice:

–Mom, Mom, don't leave me alone!

Clara and Pablo weep, pray to God, beg, send to death, complain about the Doctor, clasp their hands, despair, caress and kiss. All in vain! The sick child no longer speaks. He no longer stares, he no longer complains: he coughs, he coughs. He twists his arms as if he were going to get up, opens his eyes, looks at his father and says: –Defend me!–, he closes them again. Oh, baby doesn't talk anymore, he doesn't sees anymore, he doesn't complain anymore, he doesn't cough anymore; he's already dead!

***

Two children pass by, laughing and singing in the street:
–My New Year! My New Year!

The streetcar novel

When the afternoon gets dark and the umbrellas open, like round bat wings, the best thing the unemployed person can do is to get on the first streetcar he can find and ride through the streets, like old Victor Hugo does sitting on the imperial bus. The movement dissipates somewhat the sadness, and for the observer there is nothing more strange or curious than the series of living pictures that can be examined on a streetcar. At each step, the wagon stops, and making its way through the passengers who crowd and huddle together, an umbrella drips plentiful, and behind the umbrella, the ridiculous figure of some tired collector, drenched to the bone. The passengers ripple and divide into two compact groups, to make way for the newcomer.

Thus the waters of the Red Sea were divided so that the people of Israel could cross it on dry feet. The umbrella drains over the decking of the wagon, which gradually becomes a navigable lake. The collector shakes his hat, and a beneficent dew bathes the faces of the bystanders, as if a priest had passed through in the middle of the wagon handing out blessings with swabs. Some gentlemen sneeze. The ladies of some age raise their petticoats to a vertiginous height, so that the mud of that portable swamp does not stain them. In the street, the rain falls according to the eternal rules of the old system: from top to bottom. But in the wagon there is ascending rain and descending rain. One is, in all truth, between two waters.

I, however, spend the hours pleasantly boxed in that small Noah's ark, sticking my head out the window, not waiting for the pigeon to bring an olive branch in its beak, but to observe the delicious picture that the city presents at that moment. The wagon also takes me to unknown worlds and virgin regions. No, Mexico City does not begin at the National Palace, nor does it end at the Reforma road. I give you my word that the city is much bigger. It is a great tortoise that extends its dislocated legs towards the four cardinal points. Those legs are dirty and hairy. The City Councils, with paternal request, take care of painting them with mud monthly.

Beyond the hairdressing salon of Micoló, there is a village that lives in extravagant neighborhoods, whose names are essentially anti-aperitifs. There are very honest men who live in the square of Tequesquite, and ladies of invincible virtue whose house is located in the alley of Salsipuedes. It is not true that the barbarian Indians are camped in these exotic streets, nor is it true that the red skins make frequent excursions to the Square of Regina. The provident hand of the police has placed a gendarme in every corner. The houses in those neighborhoods are not made of mud or upholstered inside with raw hides. They are habitable houses, with stairs and everything. In them live very discreet gentlemen, and very respectable ladies, and very pretty girls. These girls usually have boyfriends, like the ones that have balconies facing the street in the center of the city.

***

After looking slightly at the crooked lines and mountain range of the new world I was passing through, I turned my eyes to the inside of the wagon. An old man with an almond-colored frock coat meditated, leaning on the grip of his umbrella. He had not shaved. His beard grew "like a poisonous grass in the sand". He probably didn't have a razor in his house... not even a peso. His frock coat needed acorn oil. However, the baldness of that respectable garment was not premature, unless we admit the theory of that young poet, author of certain verses whose dedicatory is as follows:

> *To my grandmother's untimely death,*
> *at the age of 90.*

My neighbor's frock coat was very old. As for the umbrella, we'd better not go into details. That umbrella, exposed to the elements, should have been very similar to the flags that the independents bring to light on September 15. It was a openwork umbrella, a metaphysical umbrella, proper to get wet with decency. Opened the umbrella, you could see the sky everywhere.

Who would be my neighbor? Surely he was married, with daughters. Would they be pretty? The existence of these unfortunate creatures seemed indisputable to me. It was enough to see that bald little frock coat, through which the bristles of a brush had passed, and that beautiful pair of trousers with their cute patch on the knee, to be convinced that the man had daughters. Only the women, and the fifteen year old women, know how to brush that way. When married ladies are in misfortune, they no longer take care of these delicacies and finesse. Unquestionably, that gentleman had daughters. Poor things!

They were probably waiting for him at the window, more in love than ever, because they hadn't had lunch yet. I took out my watch and said to myself: –It's four o'clock in the afternoon. Poor things! They're going to faint! I'm sure they're pretty. Their father is white, and if he were shaved, he wouldn't be so ugly. Besides, they must be good girls. This gentleman has all the appearance of a good man. I'm sorry those little girls are hungry. There won't be anything to pawn in the house, because the rents have gone up so much! Maybe they didn't have enough to pay for the house, and the landlord seized their furniture! Bad soul! These landlords are worse than Cain!

Nothing; there is no reason to dwell on the matter: the decent poor people are the worst brought and the worst taken. These girls come from a good family. They are not used to asking. They sew for peanuts; but the machines have ruined the unhappy seamstresses, and the only thing they get, at the cost of labor and work, is cheap clothes. They spend the day throwing their lungs through their mouths. And then, since they eat badly and have a lot of sorrows, they are a little sick, and the Doctor assures that, if God does not remedy it, they'll go at the fall of the leaves. They need meat, wine, iron pills and cod oil. But with what do you buy all this? The good gentleman has been laid off since the fall of the Empire, and the only son who could have been his support has both legs broken. There is no work; everything is very expensive, and friends get tired of helping the helpless. If only the girls would get married! They probably won't lack admirers. But since the poor girls are very decent and were born in good diapers, they can't fall in love with coarse men or the useless young men of the square. They are in love without knowing who, and await the coming of the Messiah. If I were to marry any of them!... Why not? After all, women who give happiness are usually to be found in that kind of people. As for the others, I know what to expect. I've had so much trouble! Nothing, the best thing is to look for one of those poor and decent little girls, who are not used to having a stage in the theater, nor carriages, nor an open account in the Surprise. If she is young, I will educate her to my liking. I'll give her a piano teacher. What is happiness? A little love, a little health and a little money. With what I earn, we can support her and me, and even the little angel God sends us. We'll love each other very much, and since I'm going to put her on a hygienic diet, she'll be cooler than a rose in no time. In the morning, a walk in the

Forest. We will go in a car of four reals[1] an hour, or in the trains. Then, in the food, a lot of meat, a lot of wine and a lot of iron. With that and with having a little house for San Cosme: with which she dresses in white, blue or pink, with the piano, books, pots and birds, I'll have nothing left to wish for.

> *An estate in the woods;*
> *A house in the estate;*
> *In the house bread and love...*
> *Jesus, what happiness!*

Besides, I have to get married. This situation cannot be prolonged, as the Grand Duke says in *The Holy War*. Here I have a hair braid that cost me four hundred and seventy-four pesos plus some pennies. I don't know where I got them from: the fact is that I had them and I don't have them. Nothing; I'll decidedly marry one of the daughters of this good man. So I take them out of sorrows and put myself in order. Which one do I marry? The blonde? The brunette? It would be better with the blonde... I mean, no, with the brunette. Anyway, we'll see. Poor things! Are they hungry?

At this point, the good man gets out of the car and goes away. If it didn't rain so much –I kept saying to myself–, I'd follow him. The truth is that my father-in-law, seen at a certain distance, has a very ridiculous face. What would he say, if she saw me beside him, Mrs. Z? His high hat looks like a mirror. Poor man! Why wouldn't she trust him? If he had asked me for something, I would have gladly given him these three coins. He's a decent person. Have those little girls eaten?

***

A thirty-year-old female now rests in the seat previously occupied by the unemployed gentleman. She has not bad eyes; her lips are thick and fleshly: they seem to have just been bitten. There are quite a few curves and no sharp angles all over her body. She has a small forehead, which I like because it's an indication of nonsense; her hair is black, her complexion is dark, and everything else is quite presentable. Who could she be? I have already seen her in the same place and at the same time two... four... five... seven times. She always gets out of the car in the square of Loreto and enters the church. However, she doesn't look like a devout woman. She does not carry a book or a rosary. Besides, when it rains like it is raining now, nobody goes to novenas or sermons. I'm sure that lady reads Gustavo Droz's novels more than Father Kempis' *Underestimation of the world*; she has a look that, if she spoke, would be a cry asking for firemen. She is covered with a black veil. In this way she protects her face from the rain. She does well. If the water falls on her cheeks, it would evaporate squeaking, as if it

---

1 Currency with different value and manufacture according to times and places.

had fallen on a hot iron. That woman is like potatoes: don't trust them even if you see them so fresh in the water: you burn your tongue.

The lady in her thirties is certainly not going to the novena. Where is she going? With a weather like this, no one leaves home except for a serious emergency. Is this lady's mother ill? In my opinion, this hypothesis is false. The lady in her thirties has no mother. The church of Loreto is neither a private house nor a hospital. Even the sacristans do not live there. We therefore have to resort to other hypotheses. It is a constant fact, confirmed by experience, that at the door of the temple, whenever the lady gets out of the wagon, she waits for a car. If the car were hers, she would come in it from her house. This has no other explanation. It belongs, therefore, to another person. Now, is there an insurance company against rain or something similar, whose members pay to have a car to the door of all the churches so that the parishioners do not get wet? Of course not. The only explanation for these streetcar trips and these prayers, at an unusual time, is the existence of a lover. Who would be the husband?

He must be a wealthy man. The lady dresses well, and if she doesn't go out in a carriage for this kind of interviews, it's because she doesn't want to be conspicuous. However, I wouldn't dare lend her fifty pesos on her word. It may well be that she spends more than she has or that she is like a certain friend of mine, a very quiet and very calm character, who told me a few nights ago:

–My wife has a prodigious fortune for gambling. Every month she gets five hundred pesos from the lottery. Fixed! –I wanted to tell him some anecdote, attributed to a well-known administrator of a certain maritime customs office. When he took care of it, he told the employees:

–Gentlemen, it's forbidden here to win the lottery. I'll kick the first one out!

Will this lady win the lottery? If her husband is poor, she must have told her that those earrings she now wears are false. The poor gentleman will not be a jeweler. When it comes to jewelry, he will only know his wife, who is a good piece jewelry[2]. Therefore, he would have believed her. How peaceful he will be in his house! Is he old? I must know him... Ah!... Yes!... That's him! No, it can't be; that gentleman's wife died when the last cholera. It's the other one! Neither! But what do I care who he is?

Will I follow her? It's always good to know a woman's secret. We will see, if possible, the incognito lover. Will this woman have children? It seems so. Infamous! Tomorrow they will be ashamed of her. Perhaps one of them will deny her. That will be a horrible crime, but a just crime. Well, let her sully, step on, spit on the honor of that wretch who probably adores her.

---

2 An ironic expression applied to a person who is naughty, cunning or vicious, with an unfavorable record.

It is a betrayal; it is a villainy. But, at last, that man can kill her, without anyone blaming or condemning him. He can send her servants to whip her, and he can tear the lover to shreds. But her children –poor helpless beings– can do nothing. The mother abandons them to go and bring them their portion of shame and dishonor. She sells them for a handful of pleasures, like Judas to Christ for a handful of coins. Now they sleep, smile, ignore everything; they are abandoned to mercenary hands; they begin to fall out of love with their mother, who does not see them, nor educates them, nor pampers them. Tomorrow those boys will be men, and those girls, women. They will know that their mother was an adventurer and they will feel shame. They will want to love and be loved; but men, who believe in the tradition of sin and in heredity, will seek them out to lose them and will not give them their name, for fear that they will prostitute and affront them.

And all that will be your work. I am tempted to go in search of your husband and bring him to this place. I can guess how is the bedroom that awaits you. Small, covered all with tapestries, with four large alabaster pitchers, holding rich exotic plants. Before there were two large mirrors on the walls; but your lover, more delicate than you, removed them. A mirror is a judge and a witness. The woman who receives her lover, seeing herself in the mirror, is already the slapped woman of the street.

Well, when you are in that warm bedroom and your lover warms your plants with his hands, numbed by the humidity, your husband and I will sneak in, and a sudden blow will throw you to the ground, while I stop the hand of your accomplice. There are kisses that begin on earth and end in hell.

***

A cold sweat washed over my face. Fortunately, we had reached the square in Loreto, and my neighbor got out of the car. I saw her dress; there was no blood on it. Nothing had happened: after all, what do I care if this lady sticks it to her husband? Is he my friend, perhaps? She is a real girl. By meeting each other we are almost friends. I already greet her.

There is the car; she enters the church; how quiet her husband must be! I'm still in the car. We all seem to be so happy!

Mylord's Revenge

To Memé

You do well to remain, hidden there, under the great chestnut trees that shade your house, eighty leagues from the dramas that Mr. Gaspar, whom neither you nor I know, makes us hear with treachery and advantage; yes, you do well. The city is sad, not because you have left it, as your boyfriend would probably tell you; the city is sad because it can't be less so, without dances, or gatherings, or shows. You, on the other hand, breathe the free air of the fields, drink light through all your pores, gallop on horseback along those shady avenues that God purposely arranged for lovers, and let your thoughts run through the countries of sleep, while here we think of building railroads and laying a network of telephone wires in the domain of owls and cats. When the evening is gathered and the stars begin to appear –as women appear on the balcony to look at their lovers– you look for the joyful stillness of the house, you open the letters of your friends, you break the yellow girdle of the newspapers, you mentally attend our theaters, and surrender to fatigue, you go to the warm bed, carrying hidden, in the small bag of your apron, the tiny sheet that you never read in front of your parents, and that you open carefully after you run the bolt of the bedroom, as if you suspected that, when you open it, the thousand kisses that your boyfriend sends you under the envelope can escape. You do well: listen to the concert of the birds, bathe in the blue waves of the pond, ride the white horse that eats in your hand sugar cubes, and read, sitting on the sidewalk in the garden, the books I send you: a novel by Halévy, the verses by Coppée and the last story by Rosa Broughton. Above all, don't read anything by Doña María del Pilar Sinués de Marco.

When the rains of September pass and the sky dresses pale blue, say goodbye to the forest, whose large trees will be left without foliage; keep in your devotional the leaves of the last heliotrope to give to your boyfriend, and go home. Then the showers and the official speeches will have passed. No one will tell you the dramatic episodes of Independence; you will be able to wear your sixteen new hats during the November festivities, and Grau –the wandering Jew– will be at the gates of Mexico. In the meantime, ride a lot on horseback, hunt with the shotgun your godfather gave you the new year, have lunch outdoors, sleep eleven hours a day and don't read the novels of Doña María del Pilar Sinués de Marco.

I am writing to you at the time when the electric light goes out and hearing the noise of the last carriages returning from the theater. I have had coffee –a coffee served by the small hand of a lady who, although beautiful, has spirit– so I'm going to spend the night awake. The new drama of Mr. Gaspar, whom neither you nor I know, has not been enough to make me fall asleep. Imagine, then, that I have gone to a dance, I have found you and we talk both under the wide leaves of an exotic plant, while the orchestra plays a waltz of Mêtra and the gentlemen go to the buffet.

If you want to, let's gossip. I'm going to talk to you about the women I just admired in the theater. Imagine that you are now in your stall and you observe through my glasses.

***

Look at Clara. That is the woman that has never loved. She has eyes as deep and as black as the opening of a mountain on a dark night. Many souls have been lost there. Out of that darkness come groans and sobs, as if from the ravine in which the Knights of the Apocalypse fatally fell. Many have stopped before the darkness of those eyes, waiting for the sudden irradiation of a star: they wanted to sound the night, and they got lost.

When the birds pass by, they say to her: Don't you love? To love is to have wings. The flowers that she steps on ask her: Don't you love? Love is the perfume of souls. And she passes indifferently, seeing with her pupils of black steel, cold and impenetrable, the wings of the bird, the chalice of the flower and the heart of the poets.

It comes from the freezing depths of the night. Her soul is like a sky without storms, but also without stars. Those who approach her, feel the cold that spreads around her a statue of snow. Her heart is as cold as a gold coin on a winter's day.

***

Who's the slender blonde smiling in that box? She is a trimmed fashion pattern. The white wings of good thoughts have never passed over that front, nor the black wings of evil thoughts. Their loves last as long as the boiling foam of champagne on the edge of the glass. She would never allow a man to hold his arms around her: she doesn't want her ribbons twisted and untidy. Do you want to know what her soul is like? Imagine a doll made of white lace, with pheasant feathers on the head and diamond eyes. When she speaks, her voice sounds like the crisp skirt of a satin tunic, grazing the marble steps of a staircase. She doesn't know where his heart is. His dressmaker never asks.

***

That serious matron sells wives. She has a lot of stock.

***

Now turn your gaze to the stall before us.

A divinely beautiful woman occupies it.

Who is she? Her big green eyes, veiled by very long black eyelashes, tremble with effusion when they look at the sky, as if they were in love with the stars. Their hands wield the fan as if they wanted to train themselves in dagger fencing. Believe it: that woman is capable of killing the man who deceives her. Her lips open softly to give way to the excess in her.

Behind the flexible rods of the corset, her heart beats in cadence; poor child who hits a wall with his little hand!

How old is she? She has turned twenty-five; I don't know how many weeks, months or years ago. As a child, a beggar who used to say good fortune, predicted that the man she loved would be terribly unhappy. Her husband, a banker, is very happy. Alicia –as it is called– is always surrounded by presumptuous wooers and fatuous lovers. When she goes for a walk, it would be said that she is a general reviewing her soldiers, who present their weapons. She, smiling, enjoying the passions she inspires without participating in them, looks out her Gioconda head through the door of the coupé and greets the platonic worshipers of her body with her gloved hand or fan. The man whom he greets with his eyes is not yet known.

Is she honest? Is she honest? Women look at her with contempt, and men court her. No one could say who her lover is or who has been; but all have the certainty that someone will be. The lottery is not done yet: the number that has to get the big prize, sleeps in the lottery balloon, confused with the others: It could be that one's, it could be mine, but it's someone's. The cage is prepared for the bird: on the sandalwood table where Alice drinks tea, there are two cups. A fool would say that one is her lover's cup. False! It's the husband's cup. When the lover arrives, Alicia and he will drink from the same cup as Paolo and Francesca read in the same book. Then they will tear it to pieces or throw it into the sea, like the king of Thulé!

The social Pimp does not err as often as some believe. What happens is that it anticipates the truth. It's like women who know the love they've inspired, half an hour before the man realizes it exists. A ship leaves the port full of goods and passengers: the sky is very blue, without a single black dot. Days and weeks go by, without the news of a storm or a squall reaching anyone's ears. And yet, one day, without knowing how or why, the voice of the shipwreck spreads. Who says so? All of them.

Who received the fatal new one? No one. Fifteen days later, the dreadful truth is known, and the newspapers refer, in detail, the horrible details of the shipwreck.

A woman is faithful to her husband. No one can accuse her of adultery. She lives, like Penelope, in her home. With arrogance she discards those who ask for her affection. But the Pimp, who looks and foresees everything, murmurs between two teams, under the wide leaves of an exotic plant erect on a rich Chinese vase: that woman has a lover! And it is not true; but one day, one week, one year later, the woman has a lover. The Pimp is just wrong in the conjugation of the verb: he should have said: she *will* have.

And the wife does not miss her duty because the world says so; as the ship does not perish because the people predict the shipwreck. Thus, the world says that Alice is disloyal, and the banned hunters are grouped around her, as the hungry castaways in the raft of Medusa. But Alicia doesn't love anyone: she keeps her treasure and doesn't want to squander it like a prodigal.

But here it is that one night a young dreamer arrives at Alicia's salon, and says to her ear:

–How you look like my first bride! She was short of stature: you are tall; she was brunette: you are blonde; she had black eyes: yours are green; but I loved her: I love you, and in this you are alike.

Two hours later, Alfredo was Alice's lover. The promised guest had arrived. The banker continued to be very happy.

Yesterday, while the husband was finishing his correspondence, Alice came out in the blue coupé pulled by two amber-colored mares. The few idlers who defied the rain on the road saw the small coupé continue its march towards Chapultepec. What was she going to do? The big cypresses, shaking their gray heads, said to each other in a low voice the secret. The mares trotted and the coupé was lost in the most shady and hidden avenue of the forest. Alfredo opened the door and took a seat next to the beautiful and coveted one. It was raining a lot. Perhaps to prevent the water from entering, wetting Alice's dress, Alfredo carefully closed the blinds. If anyone wandered through the forest at such hours, he could say to himself: Who is inside the coupé? Fortunately, the rain was getting worse and worse, and only a poor worker, hidden in the dark entrance to the cave, could see the coupé, going ahead step by step its way up the castle ramp. The mares' legs, washed and burnished by the rain, looked like golden silk.

The worker, leaving aside the sacks overflowing with strands of hay, poked his head to watch the carriage climb up to the castle gates. There it stopped: the lovers got off and twisted their steps towards the corridors, silent and desert. A carefully restrained man had climbed at the same time. After he had reached the place where the empty coupé was, he lowered the fold of his cape and made an imperative signal to the coachman, who, seeing the face of the stranger, turned pale as wax. He then got off the driver's seat, and, after very short words between them, he removed his topcoat so that the newcomer could hide with him. Half an hour later, the lovers left the castle; they got into the carriage again, and Alicia, pulling out her blonde head through the door, said: home! The mares galloped, but... Where were they going? Turning the course, the coachman led the carriage to the abyss, as if instead of going down the steep ramp he wanted to precipitate from the top of the hill. The lovers, who had closed the blinds again, could see nothing. Where were they going? Suddenly the mares stopped, as if some giant hand had grabbed them by the hooves. Whinnying they looked at the abyss that opened up to their hooves. The coupé's blinds were still closed. The coachman, standing on the driver's seat, whipped the mares; the car swung for a moment in the void, and then crashed, smashed to pieces, into the ground. Not a shout, not a complaint was heard. The coachman's body was found twenty yards away. He was Alicia's husband.

At this moment the bell rings, and that sharp sound brings me back to reality. No, it's not Alicia I'm looking at in that box. Alicia is already sleeping in the cemetery. She is a woman who looks very much like her and who will die as disastrously as she does. God confuse the cursers! Gaspar is absolutely right. The tongue kills more than the daggers. How one moralizes oneself watching these comedies!

So I already told you that this lady...

Saint John's Morning

To Gonzalo Esteva and Cuevas

Few mornings are so cheerful, so fresh, so blue, as this morning of Saint John. The sky is very clean, "as if angels had washed it in the morning". It rained last night, and dew bracelets still hang from the branches, which will evaporate after the sun shines, like dreams after dawn; the insects drown in the drops of water that slide down the leaves, and that delicious smell of damp earth is joyfully sucked in; it can only be compared with the smell of black hair, with the smell of the white epidermis and the smell of freshly printed pages. Nature also comes out of the pool with her hair down and throat uncovered; birds get drunk with water, sing a lot, and the children of the village sink their faces in the big metal basin. Oh Saint John's morning, the one with the clean shirt and perfumed soaps! I would like to look at you far away from these cauldrons in which human fat boils; I would like to contemplate you in the open air, where you still appear virgin, with very white arms and wet curls, There you are virgin: When you arrive to the city, your red lips have kissed much; many blond locks of your wavy hair have remained in the hands of your thousand lovers, as is the fleece of the lambs in the bushes of the road; many arms have surrounded your waist. You wear on your neck the red mark of a bite, and you come staggering, still with a white satin suit, but already prostituted, profaned, similar to that of Giroflé after the meal, when the bride bites her immaculate orange blossoms and soaks her hair in the wine! No, Saint John's morning, I don't want you like that! I like you in the country, where your blue eyes and your gold braids are looked at. You go down the steep hill little by little; you knock on the door or you stealthily enter the window so that your gaze illuminates the interior, and we all receive you as the sick receive health, the poor receive wealth and hearts receive love. Aren't you loving? Aren't you very rich? Aren't you healthy? When you come, the bride and the groom make their eternal oaths; those who suffer, rise up, turned to life; and the golden light of your hair sows sequins and gold coins, the dark green of the fields, the bottom of the rivers and the small table of poor wood on which the humble eat breakfast, drinking a jar of foamy milk, while the cow moans in the stable. Ah! I would like to look at you thus when you are a virgin, and kiss Ninon's cheeks... her rosy velvet cheeks and her white satin shoulders!

***

When you arrive, oh morning of Saint John, I remember an old story that you know and that neither you nor I can forget, remember? The farm where I was in those days was very big; with many bushels of land sown and countless heads of cattle. There is the house, preceded by a courtyard with its fountain in the middle. There is the chapel. Far away, under the hanging branches of the great willows, is the dam in which the flocks are to be watered. Seen from a height and from a distance, one would say that the dam is the enormous blue pupil of some giant, haphazardly stretched out on the lawn, and how deep the dam is! You know that...!

Gabriel and Carlos used to play in the garden. Gabriel was six, Carlos was seven. But one day, his mother fell into bed, and there was no one to watch their cheerful runs. It was Saint John's Day. As the evening began to decline, Gabriel said to Carlos:

–Look, Mama's asleep and we've already finished our homework, let's go to the dam. If Mom scolds us, we'll tell her we were playing in the garden. Carlos, who was the oldest, had some light scruples, but the crime was not so great, and besides, the two of them knew that the dam was adorned with large reeds and marigold branches. It was Saint John's Day!

–Come on! –He said–, We'll take a newspaper to make paper boats and we'll cut the wings off the flies to use them as sailors.

And Carlos and Gabriel went out very quietly so as not to wake their mother, who was ill. Since it was a holiday, the field was lonely. The laborers and workers took a nap in their cabins. Gabriel and Carlos did not pass through the tent, so as not to be seen, and they ran at full speed through the countryside. Very soon they arrived at the dam. There was no one, not a laborer, not a sheep. Carlos cut the newspaper into pieces and made two boats, as big as the Guatemalan ships. The poor flies, which went without wings and captive in a wafer box, humbly manned the boats. Unfortunately, the day before they had cleaned the dam, and the water was a little low, Gabriel did not reach it with his hands.

Carlos, who was the eldest, said to him:

–Let me try, I'm bigger. But Carlos couldn't reach it either. Then he climbed over the stone parapet, lifting his soles from the ground, stretched out his arm and went to touch the water and leave the boat in it, when, losing his balance, he fell into the calm bosom of the waves. Gabriel uttered a sharp cry. Breaking his nails with the stones, tearing his clothes, by force, he also managed to climb over the cornice, stretching almost the entire bust over the water. The waves were still stirring. Carlos was inside. Suddenly, he appears on the surface, with his face bruised, throwing water through his nose and mouth.

–Brother! Brother!

–Come here! Come here! I don't want you to die.

Nobody could hear. The children were asking for help, piercing the air with their cries; nobody was coming. Gabriel leaned more and more over the waters and stretched out his hands.

–Come closer, little brother, I'll stretch out to reach you.

Carlos wanted to swim and approach the wall of the dam, but he lacked strength, he was sinking. Suddenly, the waves moved and Carlos grabbed a branch, and leaning on it he managed to stand next to the parapet and raised a hand: Gabriel squeezed it with his little hands. And the poor boy wanted to raise up his brother who had lifted half a body out of the waters and was clinging to the salient stones of the dam. Gabriel was red and his hands were sweating, squeezing the brother's white hand.

–I can't get you out, I can't!

And Carlos was sinking again, and with his black eyes wide open he asked for his help.

–Don't be bad! What have I done to you? I'll give you my soldiers' boxes and the piggy bank mill you like so much. Get me out of here!

Gabriel cried nervously, and stretching more the body of his dying little brother, he said to him:

–I don't want you to die! Mom! Mom! I don't want him to die! and they both screamed, exclaiming afterwards:

–They can't hear us! They can't hear us!

–Holy Guardian Angel! Why can't you hear me?

And in the meantime, the night fell. The windows were lit in the house. There were parents who kissed their children. The stars came out in the sky. It would be said that they were watching the tragedy of those three linked little hands that didn't want to let go and were letting go! And the stars could not help them, because the stars are very cold and very high!

Gabriel's bitter tears fell on his brother's head. They saw each other, face to face, clasping hands, and one of them was going to die!

–Let go, little brother, you can't do it anymore; I'm going to die.

–Not yet! Not yet! Help! Help!

–Here, I'll leave you my watch! Here, little brother!

And with his free hand he took out of his pocket the tiny gold watch that had been given to him on New Year's Eve!

How many months had he thought tirelessly about that little gold watch! The day he finally had it, he didn't want to lie down. To sleep, he put it under his pillow, Gabriel looked with astonishment at its two covers, the white sample in which the black hands turned little by little and the instanter that, nervously, ran, ran, without ever finding the exit from the narrow circle. And he said. –When I am seven years old, like Carlos, they will also buy me a gold watch!–. No, poor boy, you're not yet seven years old, and you already have the watch. Your little brother dies and leaves it to you. What does he want him for? The tomb is very dark, and you can't see what time it is.

–Here, little brother, I'll give you my watch; here, little brother!

And the little hands, now purple, loosened, and the mouths kissed from afar. The children no longer had the strength in their lungs to ask for help, the waters are opening, as the crowd opens in procession when the Host passes by. Now they are closed and there is only one second left, on the blue wave, a straight loop of blond hair!

Gabriel started to run in the direction of the farmhouse, stumbling, falling on the stones that wounded him, Let's not say any more; when Carlos' body was found, it was already cold, so cold, that his mother, when she kissed him, she died.!

***

Oh Saint John's morning! Your white wedding dress also has blood stains!

At the racecourse

I t is impossible to separate the eyes from that long track, where the race-horses compete, marveling at their prowess. I know of many ladies who have fought with their boyfriends, because instead of seeing and admiring them, they fixed their attention on the tricks of the jockeys and on the look of the horses. And I know, however, that another friend of mine, absorbed in the contemplation of some perfectly stretched blue socks, lost his bet because he had not observed, as he should have done before, the conditions in which the race was going to take place. But this equestrian mania does not just spread among horse owners and gamblers, eager for profit; it extends to the ladies, who also follow, in favor of the telescope, the episodes and the adventures of the joust; and who bet as we bet and use in their conversation the bitter words of the equestrian language, bristling with sharp points and consonants. The gallants and the wooers will bet with the ladies, and offer a box of gloves or a case of perfume, instead of the pale camellia that withers in the lady's hair or the flirtatious gold pin that holds the curls at the nape of the neck. The brief straw goat glove that holds an ivory hand is well worth all the vases of Sévres that Hildebrand has in its luxurious warehouses and all the delicate miniatures traced by Casarín's Daudet brush. I have one of those gloves in the blue chest of my memories. Whose was it? I remember that for many days it was with me, kept in my wallet, and slept under my pillow at night. Whose was it? Poor glove! He's already missing two buttons and has a tiny tear in his little finger. It smells like blonde.

***

The arena of the racetrack has also received its baptism of blood. But who thinks during the animation of the races in those sad casts of tragedy? The horse walks arrogantly on the track, like a beautiful girl in the ballroom. He knows he's beautiful and he knows he's being watched. And the horse can kill its rider in the steeple chase, like the lady, no matter how chaste and angelic it seems to you, it can also put in your hand the vibrant foil of the duelist or the revolver of the suicidal one. All love gives death.

We caress the silky mane of the horse or we fall asleep in the shadow of a thick black hair, like the African under the perfidious frontier of the chamomile. Your legs are nervous –oh, horse–, my fingers want to hide between your manes, and when you, lengthening your noble neck, dilate your nose and run like a shot dart, I feel the palpitations of your flesh and I possess and love you, drunk with pride. I know well that in one of your jumps you can throw me to enormous distances, as a sack of bones is thrown from the top of a tower. My body will fall into the ravine or be forsaken in the plain, being the grass of the vultures. But what does it matter? I love you!

–Your eyes –oh woman– hide love at the same time as death, because they are black like night and at night pale stars and perverse malefactors reign. Your pupils give off cold lights, like steel arrows. No one has been able to surprise the hidden thoughts kept by your impenetrable forehead. You are the holy ark or the terrible Pandora's box, the condor or the worm, the summit in which one is close to the sky or the ravine whose hard ground warms the flames of hell. I have been told that I must not love you, and that is why I love you, as José adored Carmen the Gypsy. The treacherous tree raises its beautiful crown above the others: there are no nests in its branches; below is death. I can, if I wish, rest under other trees, under the honest holm oak or the hospitable walnut tree. But these do not possess your diabolical seduction, nor are they as beautiful as you. I have run the fields and the woods, weariness overwhelms me; so let me sleep under your leaves and drink the poison of death through my pores!

***

But who thinks of the mortal fall when the horse prances about, flirting in the sand of the turf nor in the tragic minute of the duel, when the dangerous beauty leans on our arm to throw herself into the fast whirlwind of the waltz? In the races I was thinking of you, oh great dominatrix, and of the bets you had made in the office. The game is the supreme sensation for those who do not know love, that other game in which the soul is bet. But the game, in the racetrack, is the game made flesh, the sensation of two thousand meters; the game with ups and downs; the game that grips its victim by the hair and swings it in space. How beautiful is "Taxatón"! Her movements are adjusted to a cadenced rhythm; the sun bathes her everywhere, she walks like a queen of fifteen years at the moment of ascending to the throne. "Jupiter" is the arrogant young man who, like Paolo, kisses the lips of the one he loves, even though he has on his chest the tip of the dagger that is going to kill him. And "Maretzek"? Where does this most noble foreigner come from? He's a nabob that walks the streets of Paris. He looks at others with arrogance and passes unperturbed, self-confident and smelling victory. But the "Eagle" does not obey the laws of gravity and seems to have wings inside, and "Caracole", crossing like a madwoman, mocks others and knows that no one can dispute her triumph. They leave now: the "Falcon" comes out shot like an enormous black stone thrown by the slingshot of a giant, and it seems that the track is rolling in front of him, like a piece of gray cloth around a rotating cylinder. "Falcon" wins until now; but the "Eagle", who has not wanted to get tired and who advances calmly, starts with an extraordinary force, taking advantage of the fatigue of his opponent, and catches him in the curve of the track, and passes him, and amidst lively and applause, arrives at the finish line without a drop of sweat, haughty and impassive like the poet who, once his tragedy is over, comes out to the stage and listens to the applause, without thanking it, as the sun does not thank the submissive looks of men.

During the fast competition, how many emotions have been felt successively by the gamblers! The money bet in the races is money that gallops and runs; you hear it coming, mounted on the horse, as if the rider had a golden armor. A lover who was next to me bet on the "Falcon" and saw him winning with horror. He had bet a box of gloves and perfumes against the blue ribbon that girded his girlfriend's throat. He wanted to lose.

In a beautiful Vigny's drama, Chatterton finds in a dance the woman he loved from afar...

...Worms of earth in love with a star!

In the tumult of the party, goes the lady who had torn his suit and looks for a pin to clip it on. Chatterton was poor but he had a very rich pin of brilliants, unique remainder of his past splendor. It was almost his entire fortune. He approached the lady and offered her the rich jewel to catch her torn skirt.

–Gentleman, I cannot receive such a priceless jewel from a stranger.

–If that's the reason, and no other –said Chatterton–, take it.

And breaking it vigorously between his fingers, he held out the pin, throwing out the window the diamonds.

***

At the racetrack I thought of nothing but the great tamer of my thoughts and the nervous agility of the "Eagle". I thought, seeing the tribunes, of the supreme painter of Parisian elegance, De Nittis. There are three pastels by De Nittis that represent several episodes of races. In one (*Pendant la Course*), the track is not seen. The painter understood that the most important in turf are not horses but women. First of all, standing on a straw chair, a tall and beautiful woman watches the race. She is in profile. I would bet she is not an honest woman.

She looks at the match coldly, as if she didn't venture a single franc of her own in it. Maybe she bet his lover's fortune. A long plush coat reaches almost to her heels, barely discovering the extremity of her Scottish petticoat. Her boots are made of gray cloth with varnished leather shoes. Her foot is not brief and her hands, hidden in the patch of skins, are not small. Her head is covered by a large myrtle velvet hat, on which a white camellia stands out, like a drop of milk falling from the breasts of Cibeles. The scene must be set in Auteuil and during the autumn races. The impassive beauty is cold. It is known in the way she ties the bridles of her hat and in the care with which she hides her throat. Next to her, but on the ground, and purposely placed to hold her in the event of a fall, is her stiff and gallant companion, arms folded across his chest. You can see the fabric of his dark suit and the fabric of his tie. One is tempted to run one's hand through the silk of the hat, to see if it gets bristled. Around, and distributed with great art, many groups of spectators are seen. Some follow with fever the incidents of the race; others engage in loving conversations; but dominating everyone, standing in the straw chair, with the same haughtiness of a statue in the marble pedestal, one pale blonde lady stands out, impassive, severe and contemptuous. Her eyes do not depart from the track. I think that with a little attention we would see the race reflected in her pupils.

In another De Nittis pastel, the scene represents a group around the brazier. The sky is dull gray, as if the snow that is going to fall in the winter were forming on top of it. In the distance you can see the track and the confused tingling of the surroundings. A group of privileged people gather around the brazier, which is an iron cone about a meter and a half long, in the center of which crackling coals burn: the red flames come out through the interstices of the fence, like the tongues of diabolical mice trying to escape from hell. Around this stove are delicious figures, whose contours swim in the light. No one thinks about horses or attends races. They all rest indolently, extending their legs to warm up to the love of fire. One can only see the foot of a character, well-shoed, whose sole is almost licked by the reddish tongues of the brazier. There is the Russian Turgueneff, a Parisian from Newskia, wrapped in the wide folds of his gown, over which the very white flakes of his beard float. Beside him, a woman, of hyperborean whiteness, looks at him smiling and showing her enameled teeth. On a chair rests and heats a woolly dog, of these that the implacable fashion shears partially, revealing his very fine pink complexion raised and the extremity of his weak legs. But the singularly beautiful figure in this painting is that of a tall and slender woman, who, leaning on the back of a chair and keeping the balance in only one foot, tends her brief sole towards the flame.

She wears a suit of dark cherry velvet and wears a hat of the same color, with blue ornaments striped in black and stopped by an airy white feather. She twists her body backwards, and as she brings his foot closer to the fire, her raised petticoat draws the morbidity of her leg. The wide and fallen brim of his hat covers a large part of her face; but you can look at the tip of the correct nose, whose rose-colored windows tremble, as if sniffing kisses, and the cut of the beard whose undulating line fades in the throat. A double blonde braid falls over the nape and escaping the tyranny of the hat. I would live under that braid.

In the air flutter, moving their sonorous elytrons, the *Hip! Hip!* of the jockeys and the *Hurray!* of the winning bettors.

***

A traveling De Nittis could find, in the stands of the racetrack, beautiful business for new paintings. Here, however, the groups are not distributed in such a picturesque and artistic way. It seems that they are all subject to the despotism of the inflexible straight line. The ladies line up in the bleachers and the men make down their sentry quarter. We don't have those horse fanatics in London and Paris either. The most famous in France is the Countess of ***, surnamed by the journalists Madame Bob. No one could say that he has been her lover, and yet the world does not judge her honest. She possesses that which Baudelaire called, with extraordinary precision, "the childlike grace of monkeys". She is thin, and when she buttons her narrow jacket on her flattened chest, one would rather believe to see a student on vacation or a jockey in a strolling suit.

Madame Bob does not boast of her titles, but she does boast of her horses, which are descended from "Gladiator" and "Lady Tempest". And they say that when she comes back from some dance, with her ivory arms uncovered and the fourteen buttons of her gloves fastened, she enters the stables, illuminated by the gas, and there she dilates her nose to feel the pungent smell of the full stables and wakes up the horses, and surrounds their necks with her arms and kisses them; and she rides like an amazon and lets herself fall between the legs of her favorite mare; and with her glossy elbow she brushes boxwood and sinks her white satin slippers into the dung, and allows the hoof of her frolicking horses to tear the crisp silk of her dress, and her thick cold mouths to wet her throat and hair. Then she goes up to her dressing table, which smells of azaleas and violets, and washes there, not in the very fine glass basins, nor in the solid silver amphoras filled with chisels and arabesques, but in the crude wooden bucket where she drenches a coarse sponge, preferring one of Santa Maria del Novella and Cyprus itself, whose smell cannot be defined, the clear water taken in the morning from the fountain, and with which it splashes, as it plunges its black curls, the walls upholstered in Japanese watercolors.

***

The horse! I understand the passions it inspires, even if they are like madame Bob's wild passion. Women love it even more than we do.

> *Come on, my intrepid,*
> *Your quick runaway*
> *Kick the ground with your foot;*
> *And your jester's snitching,*
> *Like a soldier his spear*
> *His happy parasol!*

Do you remember? It's been a long time since this: it was when you loved me. The air was fresh as if inside every drop of light was a drop of water. We had just drank in jars –you didn't want me to drink in yours– the frothy milk that was milked in front of us. How we laughed in that blue morning and how I remember the white whiskers that the milk drew on your little mouth! We were going to leave. Your horse whinnied impatiently, and your mother, on seeing him spirited, begged you not to do anything crazy. Remember? You couldn't go up, and I took you in my arms to help you. I couldn't forget it. How close we were at that moment and how far we are today! Then I fixed the long folds of your riding suit and shook in my hands your delicate shoes. You, blushing, spurred your horse and ran, laughing, across the plain. I caught up with you. We galloped a lot, a lot, towards the place where the sun rises. It seemed that we were running to a fire. The others had been left behind, and you, the frightened one, wanted us to wait for them in the shade of a tree. That's where we stopped. I was thinking of the brief shoes that your riding suit was hiding and of your little heart that I had felt next to mine. And we talked, and your golden horse came closer to mine, as if he was going to tell him some secret, and suddenly my trembling mouth kissed the delicate blond curls that stood on your neck.

How time has run! When you have daughters, don't let anyone help them to sit on their horse's saddle!

The passion of Passionflower

How the heart grieves and the spirit goes numb, when the clouds pile up in the sky, or spill their waterfalls, as the naiads pour out their rich urns! In those sad and rainy afternoons one thinks of all those who are not any more; of the friends who departed to the land of shadows, leaving at home an empty armchair and a hole that is not filled in the spirit. It seems that the heart trembles, thinking that rainwater filters through the crevices of the earth, and goes down, like crying, to the coffin, wetting the cold body of the corpses. Man never believes that life ceases; he animates with his imagination the dead body whose molecules disintegrate and enter the whirlwind of the eternal cosmos, and resists the inescapable law of beings. All of us, in our hours of sadness, when the wind blows in the narrow tube of the chimney, or when the water whips the crystals, or when we retrace with the imagination this long journey of life, the sea is agitated and turbulent; all, some more, some less, we retrace with the imagination this long journey of life, and reminding the absent, that they will never return, we believe to hear their anguished voices in the whining of the passing gust, in the rumor of the water and in the rumbling tumultuous ocean. The son then thinks of his loving father, whose gray hair is likened to the snow on the trees; the bridegroom, whose gentle lover stole the sky, thinks he hears her babbling as a child in the melancholic noise of the water; and the criminal, to whom remorse grinds, closes his ears to the robust sonority of the ocean, which, like God to Cain, says to him: Where is your brother?

And nobody thinks that those bodies are already gone and that their atoms go, wandering and scattered, from the incarnated button of the rose to the flesh of the carnivorous tiger; from the flame that oscillates in the candle to the eyes of the woman in love; nobody wants to believe that only the soul survives and that the vile matter melts; because we are so fond of the earthly envelope, and so great is the predominance of our selfish feelings that, because we have the right to imagine that our bodies are eternal, we do not consent to believe that inflexible death has finished with others, and, slandering God, we prolong life until past the yellowish shore where the domains of death begin.

This feeling is greater in those peoples that do not yet reach a higher degree of civilization and culture. The Egyptians thought that their deceased relatives would still need food. That is why they painted, inside tombs and hypogeous, servants provided with trays full of tasty delicacies, pots filled with water and big pieces of bread. Our people still preserve that superstition, and deposit, on the day of the dead, in the cemetery, what they call the offering.

***

A few days ago, I was talking to a lady about these uses and customs. The rain did not allow her to leave her house, and there, captives, we entertained the evening with tales of the appeared and resurrected.

–Do you not believe in the transmigration of souls? –she said to me.

I laughed, and pressing on her hand, I answered her:

–When I look at those eyes and that mouth, I believe in the transmigration of spirits. Cleopatra's soul lives in you, doesn't it?

My beautiful interlocutor, grateful, unraveled her brow, contracted shortly before by the sullenness of the talk, and said to me:

–I don't know if the dead return, or if souls migrate to other bodies, but I'm going to tell you a story... Juan married Antonia, as her second wife. His first wife left him a seven-year-old girl, whom his parents called Rosalía, but was called Passionflower by the neighbors of the village. Juan's first wife was all that is called an angel of God. Patient, suffering, loving, she could be seen in her husband's eyes and in the girl's fresh palmetto. The wives of the village, seeing her pale complexion, her big eyes surrounded by blue circles and the marked thinness of her sickly body, said that Passionflower's mother would not live for long. She, cheerful and resigned, waited for death singing, as the swallows await winter. One night, Andrea –it was her name– became so badly ill that there needed to call Don Domingo, the healer. All was useless! The poor mother was dying, and no one could help it. Shortly before she was in agony, she called his daughter, who was then five years old, and said to her:

–Rosalía, I'm going now. I'd like to take you, but the road is very long and very cold. Stay here; your father needs you and you'll tell him about me so he won't forget me. See you tomorrow!

Andrea closed her eyes, and Rosalía kissed her snowy hands, crying. See you tomorrow! It's true: tomorrow in heaven!

***

Juan was still young and consoled himself eleven months later. By the end of the year, he had married Antonia. This one was bad, sullen and distrustful. The stepmother –as she was called in the village– made the poor girl suffer a great deal. She treated her harshly, used to whip her when Juan was not at home, and one day she even burned his hands with a hot iron. Rosalía cried, nothing more. When her sufferings were many, she said in a low voice, with her face hidden in the corners: –Mother, mommy!

But the poor dead woman could not hear her. How heavy must be the sleep of the dead! The girls in the farmhouse, seeing her so sad, invited her to play. But she didn't go because her little shoes no longer had soles and the pebbles of the street hurted her feet. Antonia had managed to alienate her father's affection by flattering her husband. One night, Passionflower talked about her mother; but that night she was left without dinner and beaten. –Damn her, the stepmother!– said the good souls of the neighborhood. May God remember the poor Passionflower!

God has a good memory and he remembered. When no one expected it, and with no visible change in the depraved behavior of the parents, Passionflower was revived, like the wick of a lamp when the oil goes up. She was still very pale, but her eyes were as bright as the lamp that burns next to the Sacrament.

–Are you doing better, Passionflower?

–Sure I'm better, since I'm already well!

However, a doctor who was in season in the farmhouse, saw the girl and his prognosis was fatal: "She will go when the leaves fall".

Passionflower disproved this prediction with her change. Passionflower sang, while doing her household chores, whenever Antonia, lazy and selfish, was partying with the women of other farmhouses. After the stepmother arrived, Passionflower was speechless, so the birds keep quiet when they see the shotgun of the hunters! The good people of the farmhouses told themselves, with great signs of compassion, that Passionflower was crazy. They had seen her speak alone in the corners, and they had even heard these words:

–Mother! Mommy!

Passionflower was not crazy. Passionflower was talking to her mother. The holy woman, who had a chair of ivory and gold near the angels, asked for an audience with God our Lord to tell him:

–Lord, I am very happy and very rejoiced in your glory, because I am looking at you; but, if you are not angry, I will speak to you frankly. I have on earth a little piece of my soul that suffers a lot, and to suffer with her is better than to be happy alone. Let me go where she is, because the poor thing calls me and she is dying.

–Go away –said the Lord–; but if you leave, you cannot return.

–Farewell, Lord!

Glory, without its children, is no glory to a mother.

That night, Andrea appeared to her daughter and spoke to her like that:

–I told you I would come back and here I am. From now on I will not abandon you: you will give me half of the crusts of bread they give you for food, and when those evil souls whip you, we will divide the pain between the two of us.

And so it was. That's why Passionflower was happy, even if the doctor said she was dying. There is, however, no nature that can resist this mistreatment. She died when the leaves fell. Juan, who was not so bad at heart, wiped away a tear, and the priest took her to sleep in the cemetery. As it was natural, as soon as God knew about her death, he told his angels:

–Go and bring her, for here I have prepared for her a small chair made of ivory and gold, and a drawer full of toys and sweets.

The angels fulfilled his command, and mother and daughter set out on their way. But Andrea had the door to heaven closed because she was distrustful, and St. Peter, calling her aside, so that the child would not find out anything, said to her:

–You know what the master ordered: I'm sorry, old lady, but the one who goes to the fair, loses her chair.

–I already know that. I just got to the door to leave the girl there, and let her go in alone. Now that she's going to enjoy herself, she doesn't need me anymore. All I ask is that they give me a little place in Purgatory, with a window to the sky, so that I can see her from there. – St. Peter conferred with the Lord, who gave his permission, and the mother said goodbye to Passionflower.

–Mother, if you don't enter, I'll go where you go.

–Shut up, little girl, I'm just going to get your father and I'll be back soon.

Soon, yes! Passionflower is still waiting for her. The poor mother is in Purgatory, very happy to see Passionflower with the corner of her eye, playing with the angels all day long. God says that when the final judgment comes, Purgatory will end, and then the good mother will be saved. My God! When will the world end, so that these poor souls will not be separated?

The loves of the comet

olden, that's the comet's tail. It comes from the immense depths of space and has left many of their luminous locks in the crystal spikes of the stars. The coquettes want to catch him; but the comet passes impassively, without turning his eyes, like Ulysses through the sirens. Venus provoked him with her voluptuous midnight blink, as if she was already sleepy and wanted to go home accompanied. But the comet saw the winged heel of Mercury, which smiled mephistophetically, and passed very formally at the respectable distance of twenty-seven million leagues. And there you see him. I believe that in one of his journeys he found the snow star, where God's gaze never reaches, and which the mystics call hell. That's why he has spiky hair. He has seen many lands, many skies; his amorous adventures make the Seven Cabrillas laugh and when he prints his memories you will see how the planets will buy them to read them in secret, taking care that they do not fall into the hands of the little maiden stars. He's very fortunate with women: he's golden!

***

I hadn't been introduced. I usually do not receive at four thirty-two minutes in the morning; and that great noctambulist leaves his blue sheets very early, to spy on the bedroom of the dawn through the eye of the key, after the divine blonde jumps out of her bed with bare arms and loose hair. His golden pupil spies through the eastern lock. Perhaps at that instant the aurora descends the three steps of opal that its nuptial bed has, seeking to cover its numb feet with the slippers of myrtles, whose inside the angels line with white feathers detached from their wings. And he looks at her; he surrounds her with the golden fluid of his eyes; he touches her with his eyes; he feels the soft undulations of her chest; he sees how she surrounds her eyelids, discovering her pupils the color of forget-me-not and she receives in her face the first drops of dew that fall from the blonde braids, when the goddess dips her head in the great bowl of diamonds, and with the ivory comb she tidies her hair decomposed by the pillow. The comet is in love. That's why he gets up very early.

***

When the newspapers announced his arrival, I doubted his existence. I thought it was a pretext of the sun to force me to leave my bed in the early morning hours. The father of light is at odds with me because I don't make verses for him and because I don't like his daughter, the dawn.

The irreproachable whiteness of that woman despairs me; and since I love with all my soul a brunette, I hate the blondes, and especially the English. The night is brunette... Like you! Sorry! I should have said: Like you madam!

But the comet, in spite of these doubts, existed. A priest who was going to say his mass before dawn had seen him. It was not, therefore, a pretext of the boiling sun to keep me awake and take revenge on all my detours. The bakers knew him and greeted him. The great space traveler was in Mexico.

The serious observers of Chapultepec have not yet opened their lips, and keep a prudent attitude not to commit themselves. They do not yet know if this comet belongs to a good family. And they are absolutely right. You don't have to make friends with a stranger, who, judging by the trace, is an adventurous Pole. Above all, don't trust him with money. Why did he come here?

The honesty of the comet is very doubtful. It leaves at dawn from the warm dressing room in which the dawn sleeps, and not yet content to dishonor her in this way by spying through the key lock until she has just washed herself. I do not know if the dawn is harassed; but whether I know it or not, the hour when the comet leaves her house does not speak very loudly for his reputation...

The comet is no gentleman. It flaunts its beauty; it comes out with insolence, confronting the poor stars with the opulent luxury of his costume, and, without respect for the modesty of virgin stars, compromises a lady's honorable reputation. He has no shame. At the very least, he should have cloaked himself in a cape.

***

I vainly waited for the great stranger to appear in the ceiling of my bedroom. For this hiker, who does not come from Chicago, there are no notable men and no visits of etiquette. So I had to wait for him standing and armed, as a jealous man awaits his wife's lover, to say good night to him as he passes by. It was half past four in the morning. The stars whispered to each other, behind the fans, and something like a huge jet of champagne, thrown by a blue fountain, was drawn in the East. It was the comet. The moon, that great silver tray where the sun puts gold coins, was hidden, sleepless and pale, in the West. The stars and I were cold.

***

But if the comet does not now foreshadow the development of the epidemic, nor the contingency of an international conflict with Guatemala, he can collide in the dark ocean of space with this walnut shell in which we travel. Such conjecture is not absolutely inadmissible. There are 281 million probabilities against that hypothesis, but there is one in favor. If the shock paralyzed the movement of translation, everything that is not stuck to the surface of the earth would come out of it at a speed of seven leagues per second. The tenor Prats would reach the moon in four minutes. If the collision did nothing but stop the rotation movement, the seas would come out of its places and change the equator and the poles. What an admirable spectacle! The seas emptying, like plates turning over, on the land. Astronomer Wiston believes and maintains that the deluge was caused by the collision of a comet: the one that appeared again in 1680.

The bandit of space could also wrap us in his opulent tail of visitation. The comets should wear tall dresses. Unfortunately, their big golden tails, eternal desperation of actresses, sometimes are thirty and up to eighty million leagues long. If the extremity of one of those gigantic tails were to penetrate our atmosphere, charged as they are with hydrogen and carbon, life would be impossible on the planet. We would first feel an imponderable clumsiness, as if we had just had lunch in Recamier's restaurant, and then, thanks to the decrease of the azure, an immense rejoicing and a terrible nervous excitement, caused by the rapid combustion of blood in the lungs and by its rapid circulation in the arteries. We would all die laughing out loud! Servín would embrace Joaquín Moreno, and García de la Cadena, General Aréchiga.

***

But who thinks of that horrible end of the world, oh my life?

The smell of roses is short-lived and champagne evaporates into impalpable atoms, if we leave it, forgetful, in the glass. Our affection flies to where the notes that are lost, groaning, in space go. Tomorrow you will have gray hair and I will have wrinkles. On your knees your kids will jump happily. Don't worry: we have time to love each other, because love doesn't last long. Close your balconies at night so that the impertinent light of the dawn does not enter very early, and try to ignore your foresight, so that you do not guess the disappointments and disappointments that the future brings us. The world is old, but we are young. When you are at a dance, never think of the daybreak or the cold of the exit, for your bare shoulders will tremble, as if feeling the rough contact of a wind of December, and you will feel the imprudent yawn of annoyance rising to your throat. The sperm candle shine, and there is much light in the mirrors, in the diamonds and in the eyes. Music frolics in space, and the waltz, like the blue wave of a German river, drags the closely united couples like the bodies of Paolo and Francesca.

The glasses of Bohemia overflow with wine that gives warmth to the body, and the half-open mouth of the woman spills these words that give warmth to the soul. In the meantime, the dawn waits and thinks of rising. Let us not think of her. Outside there is a cold wind that tears the naked flesh of those poor people who have spent the night begging and return home without a single crust of black bread.

Do not think, for God's sake, of the hood of heavy skins that sleeps waiting for you in the cloakroom, nor of the closed windows of your carriage. The end of the world and the beginning of a dance is all one. The end of the feast mixed with silence and fatigue, the time when the years are extinguished and everyone returns home; the former to sleep under the quilted clothes of their bed, and the latter to rest between the four walls of the tomb. The candles sputter, licking the borders of the coiled candelabra; the buffet turkeys show their gnawed shells and their open bellies; the musicians, struggling with sleep, like Jacob with the angel, find no air in their lungs to throw it through the sharp clarinet, nor vigor in their loose articulations to wield the violin bow; on the white canvas that covers the carpets there are many trampled flowers and many shattered laces; the women are getting haggard, and the rice dust falls, like the pollen of a flower, from their cheeks; the coachmen, immobile, sleep on the coachman's seats wrapped up to the forehead with their overcoats; this is the end of the dance, this is the end of the world. But –wait a moment– the cotillion is missing!

> *Let's stay! The star wanders,*
> *Whose wise men are afraid of the distance,*
> *Maybe, by taking the world away,*
> *Will leave us in our corner!*

***

The comet doesn't come to exterminate us. He continues to shake his Merovingian hair before the respectable face of the moon, and continues his adventures like Don Juan. He throws a lunge to Mars and slips like an eel through Saturn's rings. Look at him! He keeps lacing in space, bombarded by the glances of the Bear. He rests in Casiopea's chair and is busy honing Sobieski's brilliant shield. The peacock unfolds the fan of his tail to make him fall in love, and the Indian bird will stand on his shoulder. The Southern Cross opens its arms to him, and the Grebes march obedient to his side. There is Orion, who greets him with his eyes, and the fatuous Arthur seeing himself in the mirror of the waters. He can curl Berenice's hair, and go, rider on the Girafa, through the northern Triangle. The Lion throws himself at his feet and the Centaur follows him at a gallop. Hercules presents his mace and Andromeda calls him tenderly. The Milky Way stretches out a white carpet at his feet, dotted with glittering sequins, and the Pegasus leans over to be mounted.

But you will not possess it, oh stars in love! He already knows what other of his companions have been lost by getting too close to the planets. Like men when they fall in love, they have married. They lost their independence since then, and today they gravitate following a tight curve or an ellipse. That's why he flees and dodges your golden nets; it's the dawn! Look at him spying on his beloved blonde by the shining lock of the East. The sky begins to blush. It's already daylight! The stars are extinguished in the sky, and the eyes that I love are opened on earth.

After the races

When Berta put her silver hairpins and ruby earrings on the marble table, the bronze clock, surpassed by the image of Galatea sleeping among the roses, struck twelve bells with its sharp chime. Berta let her blond Venetian braids kiss her waist, trembling, and extinguished the candle with her breath, so as not to see herself undressed in the mirror. Then, stepping on the forget-me-not of the carpet with her bare feet, she went to the narrow bed of rose-colored wood, and, after a very brief prayer, she reclined on the white bedspreads that smelled of new linen and violet. In the warm bedroom one could hear the stealthy footsteps of the elves who wanted to see Berta asleep and the ticking of the tireless pendulum, eternally in love with the hours. Berta closed her eyes, but did not sleep. Through her imagination, the horses of the racetrack crossed swiftly. How beautiful is life! A house covered with tapestries and surrounded by a belt of white camellias in the corridors; below, the carriages, whose shining varnish wounds the sun, and whose interior, padded and warm, transcends the skin of Russia and goat; the horses that stamp in the wide stables and the beautiful banana leaves, erect in Japanese vases; above, a blue sky of new satin, much light, and the notes of the birds rising, like crystal souls by the flowing amber of the atmosphere; inside, the father with white hair who never finds enough pearls or enough lace for his daughter's wardrobe; the mother who watches over her bedside when she is ill, and who wants to surround her with cottons, as if she were made of brittle porcelain; the children who moved naked in their cradle, and the clear mirror that smiles on the marble of the toilet. Outside, in the street, the movement of life, the coming and going of the carriages, the bustle; and at night, when the dance or the theater ends, the figure of the poor lover who waits for her and who walks away satisfied when he has seen her get out of his carriage or closing the doors of the balcony. Lots of light, lots of flowers and a new silk suit: that's life!

***

Berta's thinking about racing. "Caracole" had to win. In Chantilly, not long ago, she won a prize. Pablo Escandón would not have given eleven thousand pesos for a bad mare and a bad horse. In addition, the person who bought the mare in Paris was Manuel Villamil, the Mexican most expert in this kind of sport. Berta is going to make a formal bet next Sunday with her father: bet on Aigle; if she loses, she will have to embroider some slippers; and if she wins, they will buy for her the mirror that Madame Drouot has in her dresser. The frame is lined with blue velvet and cuts the mirror moon obliquely, under a garland of flowers. How beautiful it is! His face reflected in that mirror will look like that of a houri, who, opening the roses of paradise, looks at the world!

Berta squints her eyes, but immediately closes them again, because the bedroom is in the dark.

The elves, eager to see her asleep, to kiss her on the mouth, without feeling it, begin to surround her with poppies and burn opium grains in small bowls. The images vanish and fade into Berta's imagination. Her thoughts sputter. She no longer sees the racecourse, bathed in the shining light of the sun, nor sees the judges perched in their praetorium, nor hears the cracking of the whips. Two figures remain only in the crystal of her memory, tarnished by the breath of dreams: "Caracole" and her boyfriend.

> *Now everything lies in unarmed repose;*
> *The blue lily sleeps in the window;*
> *Do you hear, from his tower the bell*
> *Midnight announces: sleep, sleep.*

***

The frolicking genius who opened Berta's bedroom for me, as a box of sweets opens on New Year's Day, put a finger on my lips, and holding my hand, led me through the halls. I was afraid to stumble upon some piece of furniture, waking up the servants and the owners. I passed with caution, holding my breath and almost sliding on the carpet. A little while later, I hit the piano, which complained in si bemol; but my companion blew, as if he were to turn off the light of a candle, and the notes fell silent on the carpet;

the breath of the genius had broken those soap bubbles. In this guise we passed through several rooms, the dining room, in whose walls, covered with walnut, thick candelabras with extinguished sperm candles could be seen; the corridors, full of pots and filigree aviaries; a passage as narrow and long as a canyon, which led to the rooms of the servants; the twisted snail through which one climbed to the roofs and a labyrinth of small rooms, full of furniture and useless junk. At last, we arrived at a small door through whose lock a ray of dim light filtered. The door was locked from the inside, but nothing resists the finger of the geniuses, and my companion, entering through the eye of the key, removed the latch that locked the door. We entered: there was Manon, the seamstress. An open book spread its white pages on the floor, barely covered with broken mats, and the candle died licking the edges of the candlestick with its salamander tongue. Manon was surely reading when the dream surprised her. That imprudent candle that could have caused a fire was proof of that, the ill-treated volume that lay next to the iron cot, and that bare arm that, in the cold of the marble, hung out of the mattress and between the disordered clothes. Manon is as beautiful as a sick lily. She is twenty years old, and she would like to read life, just as she wanted as a child to leaf through the engraving volumes that her father kept. But Manon is an orphan and poor: she will no longer see, as before, around her, obedient waitresses and submissive domestics; they have left her alone, poor and sick, in the middle of life. From that previous life which, at times, she feels like a dream, all she has left is a complexion that still transcends almond, and a hair that still hunger, misery and work has not turned harsh. Their thoughts are like those enchanted children that appear in the stories: they walk by day with their feet bare and dressed in a shirt; but let the night come, and you will see how those poor beggars wear jackets of crisp silk and adorn themselves with feathers of pheasants.

That afternoon, Manon had attended the races. In Berta's house everyone loves and pampers her, as one loves and pampers a lapdog, dressing it in wool in winter and giving her biscuits soaked in milk. Everyone knew the condition that this humble seamstress had had before, and they treated her with great delicacy. Berta gave Manon her old dresses, and used to take her when she went for a walk or to shops. The orphan received these tokens of affection as the poor beggar receives the coin that a pious hand throws from a balcony. Sometimes these coins are prejudicial.

That afternoon Manon had attended the races. They left her inside the carriage, because it doesn't feel good for an aristocratic family to go for a walk with the maids; they left her there, in case the girl's dress was torn or if the ribbons of her "hood" were broken. Manón, glued to the windows of the carriage, was spying there on the track and the stands, just as a poor little sick woman sees, through the windows of the balcony, the life and movement of the passers-by. The horses crossed like exhalations on the arid track, stretching out their bristly manes in the air. The horses! She, too, had known that pleasure, half spiritual and half physical, which is experienced when galloping through a sandy avenue. The blood runs faster and the air whips as if it were angry. The body feels youth and the soul believes it has regained its wings.

And the grandstands, seen from afar, seemed to her like enormous bouquets made of satin leaves and carnations of meat. The silk caresses like the hand of a lover and she had an infinite desire to feel that contact again. When the woman walks, her skirt sings a hymn in her praise. When could she hear those verses? And she saw her hands, and the tip of her fingers mistreated by the needle, and stubbornly fixed herself on that picture of splendors and feasts, as on the night of Saint Sylvester the poor children see those cakes, those sweets, those candy pyramids that they will not savor and that adorn the candy shop windows. Why was she banished from that paradise? Her mirror said to her: "You are young and beautiful". Why did she suffer so much? Then a voice rose within her, saying, "Do not envy such things. The silk tears, the velvet is crushed, the epidermis wrinkles with age. Under the blue surface of that lake there is a lot of mud. All things have their bright side and their dark side. Remember your friend Rosa Té? Well, she lives in that theater sky so full of talcum powder and tinsel and painted canvases. And the husband who she chose, deceives her and flees from her side to run after women who are worth less than her. There are silk shrouds and coffins of guayacan, but in all of them the worms tingle and bite".

Manon, however, longed for those triumphs and those finery. That is why she slept dreaming of rejoicing and parties. A gallant, similar to the wandering knights who appear in German legends, stopped under her windows, and, climbing a blue silk ladder, reached her, girded her tightly with his arms and then went down, bending in the air, to the shadow of the olive grove stretched out below. A horse waited there. And the gentleman, carrying her in his arms, as if he were carrying a sleeping child, was riding on the spirited colt that ran at full speed through the woods. The mastiffs of the farmhouse barked and even the windows were opened, and in them appeared fearful faces; the trees ran, ran in the opposite direction, like a defeated army, and the knight pressed her against his chest, curling with his burning breath the thin hairs of her neck.

At that moment the dawn came out of its dewy marble tub fresh and perfumed. Do not enter –oh cold light!–, do not enter the alcove where Manon dreams of love and wealth! Let her sleep, with her white arm hanging out of the mattress, like a virgin who has gotten drunk on the water of roses. Let the stars come down from the blue sky, and latch onto her tiny ears of transparent porcelain.

The daughter of the air

I seldom go to the circus. Every spectacle in which I look at human abjection, whether moral or physical, disgusts me greatly. Some nights ago, however, I entered the tent set up in the Seminary square. An acrobat dislocated himself making grotesque contortions, exploiting his ugliness, his shamelessness and his idiocy, like those beggars who, in order to stimulate the long-awaited generosity of the passers-by, show their wounds and exploit their rottenness. A woman –almost naked– twisted like a snake in the air. Three or four Herculean muscle gymnasts threw great weights, bronze balls and iron bars at each other. How much degradation! How much misery! Those men had renounced the noblest thing God has given us: thought. With the smile of the cretin they see the public kicking, howling and stimulating them with their voices. They are his beast, his thing. Some night, in the middle of that sanded roundabout, in the light of the gas lamps and among the sounds of a bad band of street musicians, they will fall from the vacillating trapeze, they will hear the cry of supreme terror that the spectators launch in the paroxysm of delight, and they will die bathed in their own blood, without tears, without pity, without prayers.

***

But what upsets my thoughts the most is the unworthy exploitation of children. A few nights ago, a girl fell from the horse she was riding and was about to be horribly trampled. Remember the poor daughter of the air, who came to the same circus a year ago? I can still see her: the clown rolls in the sand, saying insulting buffooneries; all of a sudden I see a weak, small and sick being climbing up the cable flywheel that ends at the trapeze bar. It's a girl. Her thin arms are perhaps going to break; her neck is going to break and her blonde head will fall to the ground, like a lily whose thin stem was blown off by the wind. How old is she? Oh, it's almost impossible to read the number of years on that pale forehead, on those dull eyes, on that deformed body! It seems that these children are born old.

She is already climbing the bars of the trapeze: the torture has already begun. That small body is uncoiled and twisted, spins like a banderilla, hangs from the thin tip of her feet, and, by a miracle of equilibrium, is held in the air, stopped by her tiny heels that stick to the moving bar. At times, I can only see a floating blonde hair, loose like Ophelia's, spinning and spinning in the air. It would be said that the blood flees in terror from that fragile body that has the whiteness of the asphyxiated, and takes refuge only in the head. The audience applauds... No woman cries, I have seen so many cry for the death of a canary!

***

When the torture is over, the girl comes down from the trapeze, and with her portraits in her hand she begins to walk around the boxes and the stands. She begs. She passes close to me: I stop her.

–Are you ill?

–No, but it hurts a lot...

–What hurts you?

–Everything.

The light in her pupils burns dimly, like the light of a dying firefly. Her thin lips open to give way to a groan, which no longer has the strength to go out. Her arms are thin, pale, bloodless. She is the daughter of pain and sadness. So pale and so sad was the girl I watched in agony, and whose image was engraved forever in my memory. For her, childhood has no rosy hues, no games, no caresses, no joys. No: it is the soul that comes; it is the soul that goes away.

***

Say, poor child, what, you have no mother? Were you born of a passionate woman, or did you come to earth in a pale moonbeam? If you had a mother, if you had been snatched from her arms, she, with that incomparable divination that love gives us, would know where you cried and suffered; crossing the seas, the mountains, she would come like a madwoman to free you from this slavery, from this torment. No, there are no bad mothers; it is a lie. The mother is God's projection on the earth. You are an orphan.

Why didn't you die when you were born? Why do you walk barefoot through that hard country of suffering? Say, poor child, what, you don't have a guardian angel? You are very sad; no one sweetens your sadness. You are sick: no one heals you or caresses you softly. Ah, how you will envy those happy and blessed girls who come to see you, next to their parents! They have not felt how the strong hand of a soulless gymnast breaks the bones, breaks the tendons and dislocates the legs and arms, until turning them into elastic easels of rag! They haven't felt how the whip of the trainer who punishes you is turned into live flesh. For them there is no hard work; there are no twists and turns on the fixed bar. They have a mother!

Say, poor child: why don't you detach yourself from the trapeze to even die and rest? You, you sick white, sad, you wander your gaze languidly. How you must hate us, poor child! You will think that men are monsters without pity, without heart. Why do they allow this most bloody torment? Why don't they pick me up and give me, since I am an orphan, that divine mother called the Holy Charity? Why do they pay my executioners and entertain their idleness with my sorrows? Oh, poor child, you can never complain to anyone. Since you have no mother on earth, you do not know God and you do not love Him. They call you daughter of the air; if you were, you would have wings; and if you had wings, you would fly to heaven!

***

Poor daughter of the air! Perhaps she sleeps now in the common grave of the cemetery! The child martyr of the season does not work on the trapeze, but on horseback. Everything is one and the same.

I hear with insistence that it is now necessary to organize a society that protects animals. Who will protect men? I admire that supreme piety, which extends to the mule that is overwhelmed by the weight of its load, and the bird whose flight cuts through the lead of the hunters. That great redemption that frees all slaves and undertakes a crusade against barbarism is worthy of approval and increase in value. But who will free those poor beings that parents corrupt and prostitute, those martyred children whose existence is a very long ordeal, those unfortunate ones who travel the three great hells of life: Illness, Hunger and Vice?

Tragedies of actuality

RENTING A HOUSE

Characters

The owner: fat man, good color, low stature and of a somewhat romping nature.

The tenant: young, skinny, very capable of making verses.

The lady: matron with good flesh, although a little tricky.

Seven or eight children: mute characters.

SINGLE ACT

The owner: Are you, sir, the one who wants to rent the upper floor of the house?

The would-be tenant: A servant of you.

–Ah! Ah! Pancracia! Children! Here is the gentleman who is going to take the house. (The family gathers around the foreigner and examines him, giving signs of curiosity, mixed with a wisp of commiseration.) Now, my sons, you have seen him well; so let me question him alone.

–Question me?

–Tell the doorman to close the door tightly and not to let anyone in. Gentleman, take a seat.

–I wouldn't want to disturb... if you're busy...

–No way, no way; take a seat.

–I can come back...

–No way. It's a matter of very brief moments. (looking at him) The face is not so bad..., good eyes, well-toned voice...

–The doorman had told me...

–Excuse me! Excuse me! Let's go by parts! What's your name?

–Carlos Saldaña.

–From Saldaña?

–No, no, sir, just Saldaña.

–Bad, bad! He would have given some distinction to the surname. If you rent my house, you must add that particle to your name.

–But, sir!

–Nothing, nothing: this is done every day and everywhere; you won't want to deny me that service. That gives credit to a house... Let's continue.

–I'm thirty years old, I'm single.

–Single? Everything that is called a bachelor? I am neither rigorous nor a maniac: I still remember my youth; I wouldn't dislike to find pretty little palms on the stairs; the sound of silk brings better days to my memory?

But, let's keep the moral high, above all!

–But, my lord...

–Yes, I know what you're going to say to me: that this doesn't concern me, that no one gives me a candle at this funeral; but, look at you for example, I'd be terribly upset if your girlfriend were a brunette...

–I repeat that...

–Be calm; it will be a weakness, I confess, but brunettes disgust me! I can't stand them. So let's sit down and let's say that, if the house suits you, you are obliged in writing to make all your girl friends very blonde. Do you have a profession?

–None.

–I'm celebrating it. It's the best guarantee that the tenants won't make noise.

–I dedicate myself to taking care of my interests...

–We'll talk about that: I'll introduce you to my lawyer.

–Thank you. I have mine.

–It doesn't matter, you'll change as soon as you move in. I have solemnly promised my lawyer to give him the clientele of my tenants. What about health?

–Me, well, what about you?

–No, I'm not saying that: what I'm asking is what your temperament is. Are you lymphatic, sanguine, nervous?

–Lymphatic..., I think lymphatic.

–Well, you get naked!

–What...?

–For a moment. It is an indispensable formality. I don't want my tenants to be sick.

–But...

–Let's go! The other sleeve, bad, bad! You didn't look so skinny. Do you know how much you weigh?

–No.

–The neck is short... Oh, my God! Those veins; be very careful with the stroke!

–Won't we finish?

–You'll have to formally commit yourself to take a purge at the beginning of each season. I will indicate to you the apothecary where you must buy it.

–Can I wear the coat?

–Wait a minute. Don't you exercise?

–I go round the Alameda eleven times in the afternoons.

–That's too little. From now on you will live in the countryside three months each year. That's good for the ventilation of the houses and for the staircase to be kept in good condition. We always travel in autumn.

So we said thirty-five pesos...

–What?

–I confess to you that the rent seems to me a little exaggerated...

But man, it doesn't matter! Everything will be discussed! Let's go by parts!

–But...

–Do you think renting me a house is the same as buying a pair of trousers? You go down the street, look at the card, go up, sit next to me, and only three minutes have passed when you ask me for the keys.

I like frankness! Why don't you ask me for my robe and slippers?

–I didn't know...

–These matters are usually treated with unforgivable lightness.

Returning, then, to our business, I will tell you that I will not ask a single real more than thirty-pesos.

–Gentleman, not another word, or I'll send my godparents to you! Well, that was all there was to it! Do you perhaps know the conditions of the lease?

–No, but I am ready to subscribe to them as long as they are just and rational.

–Listen to me:

Art. 1° The tenant will go to bed at the same time as his owner, so as not to disturb the latter's rest, which precisely occupies the mezzanine.

Art. 2° The tenant will invariably wear light suits so as not to upset the owner's mood, if by chance he finds him on the stairs.

Art. 3° The tenant will appear on the balcony at least twice a day, rubbing his hands with satisfaction, in order to prove the good order and excellent service of the house.

–And when it rains?

–He'll look out with an umbrella... I continue. The tenant will never enter the house without a certain complacency in the details of the architecture, nor will he be embarrassed at all to make clear, in a loud voice, his enthusiasm for the facade. The more people he gathers, the better.

Art. 4° The tenant will invite the owner to eat every 15th day, taking care, of course, not to take him to any restaurant or second-class inn.

Addition to Art. 4° These monthly meals have for object the tightening of the friendships between tenant and owner. It is not forbidden to the tenant to be accompanied by his girlfriend.

Art. 5° The tenant will greet very politely the janitor, who is cousin, by affinity, of the owner.

Art. 6° The artists and writers who come to visit the tenant will climb the access stairways.

–Is there no more, sir?

–There are still some additional articles which I will make known to you in due course.

–Well, everything is very fair and very sensible...

–I forgot... Aren't you a Mason?

–No.

–Well, I'm sorry. My wife is very anxious to know the secrets of the Masons.

–If you like, I'll have them present me in some lodge.

–I would appreciate that very much.

–So we agreed that thirty pesos...

–Excuse me...

–Still more?

–I forgot to ask you, why did you leave your old home?

–Me, for nothing! Because I threw the owner off the balcony.

Christmas Masses

I went for a walk in the streets for a while, and everywhere, the fresh smell of moss, the bustle and noise of the squares and the eternal fuss of the whistles have tied my thoughts to Christmas Eve. It is impossible for us to talk about anything else. The barracks scattered miserably in the Main Square have been more animated this afternoon than ever. The street vendors could not stop for an instant. At every step I stumble upon human mules, laden with heavy baskets, on whose borders protrude the outstretched arms of a cedar branch, or the gray strands of hay. At times, breaking the monotony of that human mass dressed in rags, an aristocratic armour and a Devonshire hat appear. Holding his sister's hand, a three-year-old boy goes by, looking at each thing with eyes wide open, and shouting with joy, like pearly notes, whose unruly compass he carries with his fleshy impatient hands. The light of the bonfires and of the torches, flaming quickly, communicates to the faces that purple reflection that illuminates the Venetian paintings. There I distinguish the slender and elegant body of Miss C..., the queen of aristocratic thinness, covered by a pearl silk dress with large black stripes. She carries a child by the hand, and, curving her body gracefully, she waits for the salesman of toasted face and thick hands to fill the basket that holds a lackey in his arms. She is Juan Goujon's Diana in the market.

A ragged crowd circulates laboriously through the square. The screams of the peddlers, who preach their wares, stun the ear, together with the intemperate whining of some whistles, similar to the sour crunch and scraping of a silk skirt when torn. The chlorotic candles that illuminate the barracks spread a yellowish light, which contrasts with the radical red of the torches. From time to time a carriage approaches, it arrives, stops, the lackey jumps of the running board, the door opens, the footboard falls and a perfectly imprisoned foot in an irreproachable booty touches the ground. Behind the girl that has first jumped from the carriage, and whose face we are accustomed to look at in the walking booth of the promenade and in the box immobile of the theater, the little brothers and the mother descend, advancing step by step. At a respectful distance, and hanging an enormous basket on his arm, comes the lackey with his withered-leaf-colored livery.

The same animation reigns in the streets. The boxes remain open and the sideboards illuminated until late at night. It is hardly possible to walk on the sidewalks. Some mistresses, who have been surprised by the night, trot, fearing to arrive too late, because of the bundling, pulling the hand of the lazy child who refuses to walk fast. Next to the glass of each sideboard, the curious passers-by gather and stare at the microscopic sperm candles, which have exhausted all the colors of the iris, the capricious and grotesque toys, and the New Year's boxes and gifts.

The cold air that hits our faces seems to be saying to my ears: "Come on, you fool! The night is going to be freezing; the frozen air clouds the crystals; it tempts the leaves of the rose bush, they are already wet like the lips of the child when he releases the mother's plentiful breast, each one takes refuge in his little house, where there are blue eyes and blond hair next to the fire: this is the home party, the grandfather's party, the wife's party, the children's party; the patriarchal supper that gathers everyone under the rough oak table is the great symbol of the family created by the Gospel. Do you not hear the cries of joy that escape through the joints of that poorly closed blind? Do you not see the restless flames of the candles, lost, like fatuous fires, in the dark branch of the Noel tree? Sad of those who run the streets with their overcoats buttoned, looking through the cracks of the doors at the fire of a festive home! Sad of those who do not have a Noel tree!"

Christmas night is the night of resurrections and memories. The children, falling asleep in their cribs, are confident in the mysterious spirit that will descend during sleep to fill with sweets and toys the new boots they have deliberately left in the chimney. The fairy who visits these booties is called in Italy the fairy Befana. In Germany, far from the big cities, in the villages of peasants and bourgeoisie, the girls lean out at the sound of twelve o'clock at night at the well, whose murky waters shine like a sick pupil, to look for, traced on its surface, the image of their boyfriends. The villagers who return to their houses, after hearing the midnight mass, discover almost always between the dark frontier of the trees, the white and agile body of the willis[1], which are delivered to an endless waltz. The midnight mass! I know of a legend that Alphonse Daudet has collected in one of his works, and that makes the good peasants who listen to it with their bristly hair open their eyes out of all proportion.

Imagine that you are in a sacristy full of spider's webs, and that you hear this dialog:

–Two truffled young goats, Garrigú?

–Yes, Reverend Father, two young goats; two young goats full of truffles. I helped to fill them myself. Their skin, strongly stretched, snapped with anguish when they entered the oven.

Garrigú..., the surplice! My God! I'm delirious for truffles! Two young goats, eh? And what else?

–The most appetizing and exquisite. Since the morning we've only been plucking pheasants, turkeys and pigeons. A cloud of feathers, dancing through the air, surrounded us constantly. Then came the eels, the golden carps and the trout.

–Trout, huh? And what size?

–Huge, Reverend Father, huge!

–Oh, my God, I can see them! Have you filled the cruets yet?

–Yes, Reverend Father, but that sad wine can't be compared to the one you'll enjoy at the end of the mass, in the castle. If you saw in the dining room the jars and carafes that shine, filled to the brim with exquisite wine... And the silverware, the chiseled fountains..., and the flowers, the candlesticks!... You could never, ever have tasted a better dinner! The Marquis has invited all the nobles who live nearby; forty, not counting the tabellion, will come to the table. How fortunate you are, my Reverend Father!

Only having felt the smoke of the truffles, their roguish smell follows me everywhere...

–Come on, come on, my son! God preserve us from gluttony, and especially on Christmas Eve! He lights the candles and gives the first touch of Mass. Midnight is almost upon us, and we must not be a moment late.

They were holding this talk on a Noel night in the year of grace of one thousand and six hundred and many, the Reverend Don Balaguer, former prior of the Barnabites, then the retired chaplain of the high and powerful lords of Trinquelag, and his assistant Garrigú, or, to put it better, the one that Don Balaguer took for his assistant Garrigú; as will be see later, the devil had taken that night the round face and indecisive features of the young sacristan to induce the Reverend Father into temptation and make him commit the ugly sin of gluttony. So, in the meantime, the one who was called Garrigú. (Hmm!, hmm!), ringed the bells relentlessly, awakening the modest echoes of the feudal castle, the reverend finished covering his cha-

---

1   White female spirits wandering through the forest at midnight like ghosts, tormenting the men who get lost in the wilderness.

suble in the small sacristy, already somewhat restless by these gastronomic temptations, and repeating to himself, mentally:

–Two truffled young goats! Turkeys! Carps! Trout! Meanwhile, the end of the night complained outside, the joyful music of the bells crumbling in the space. Little by little, vague lights were emerging from the shadow, on the arid slope of the mountain, approaching the heavy feudal factory. They were the families of the peasants who came to Midnight Mass in the castle. Gathered in groups of six or seven, they climbed singing, on the rocky slope, guided by the father who, lantern in hand, was lighting his way. The children, huddled together with the mothers, took shelter with their loose brown blankets. In spite of the hour and in spite of the cold, all those people were rejoicing and very happy, sure that once the services were finished, they would find in the castle's kitchen the table that was served every year. From time to time, interrupting the painful march, the groups separated to let the free passage to some carriage, which, preceded by four beaters, with torch in hand, made gleam its diaphanous crystals wounded by the moon. Moments later, an obedient mule, who made his bells rattle, trotted along with the villagers. By the light of the lanterns, circled in mist, the peasants recognized the mayor.

–Good night, Mr. Mayor!

–Good night, good night, my children!

The night was clear; the cold stirred up the shifting glow of the stars; the north wind scraped the skin hard, and a faint frost, slipping on the dresses without wetting them, sowed like little pinheads on the heavy woollen blankets, and faithfully preserved the tradition of Christmas, white with snow. Above the mountain appeared the castle as the end of that walk, with its enormous mass of towers and pinions, with the bell tower of its Gothic chapel, piercing the blue of the sky, and with the crowd of impatient lights, that blinked, went and came shaking in all the windows, similar, on the shady bottom of that factory, to the sparks that run and are reached in the ashes of the burnt paper. Passing the drawbridge and the postern, it was necessary, to enter the chapel, to cross the first courtyard all full of carriages, lackeys and bunk beds, illuminated by the fire of the torches and the reddish glow of the kitchen. In that courtyard you could constantly hear the tinkling of the grill, the din of the pots and pans, the shock of the crystals and the silverware. All these preparations of the dinner and the warm steam that reached his senses, transcending to well roasted meats and sauces of odorous legumes, made the peasants say, like the chaplain, like the mayor:

–We are going to have a good dinner after mass!

The first midnight mass has begun. In the chapel of the castle, an entire miniature cathedral, with intertwined arches and rare walnut woods that climb all the way up the walls, all the tapestries have been unrolled and all the candles lit. How many devotees! What a multitude of costumes! Behold, first, the high and mighty lord of Trinquelag, with his taffeta salmon dress, accompanied by the noble lords invited, girded in the sculpted masonry of the choir. A little further on, kneeling in large reclinatories clad in thick velvet, the widowed Marquise, in her fire-colored brocade costume, and the young lady of Trinquelag, combed with a tower of lace in the latest court fashion, pray devoutly. Further down rise mourners, with their bearded cheeks and immeasurable wigs, Mayor Thomas Arnoton and the Maese tabellion Ambroy; two serious notes lost between the dazzling silks and the spurred damask. Then, standing out, the butlers, the pages, the tamers, the wardens, Mrs. Barba with her bunch of keys, hung at the waist by means of a silver burnished ring. And down to the bottom, in the pews for the people, the servants, the peasants, the plebeians, still escorted by a multitude of chef's assistants, that in the end of the chapel, next to the high door, opening and closing at every moment, come to hear some verse of the trades and to bring, I do not know why, a vague smell of supper to that church dressed up for a festivity, and whose atmosphere warms the red flames of the candles.

Is the presence of those white aprons the cause of the officiant's involuntary distractions? What is certain is that the mischievous bell, moved by the sacristan with a diabolical precipitation, seems to be saying with a sharp voice: "Let's go! Let's go! The sooner you pray, the sooner we sit at the table".

And the fact is that every time it rings –mischievous bell!– the chaplain forgets the mass so as to think only of dinner. And he imagines the incessant movement that there must be in the kitchen, the ovens where the fire of the forge flames and collides, the smoke that the ajar lids let escape, and through that smoke he looks at two magnificent young goats, with truffles.

Or he watches the rows of colorful young pageboys pass by, prudently carrying plates encircled by tempting smoke, he enters with them into the room already prepared for the party and –oh delight!– here is the immense table all resplendent, already loaded with the turkeys dressed with their feathers, the pheasants opening their wings, the ruby-colored bottles, the pyramids of fruits standing out among the green branches, and, finally, those prodigious fish of which Garrigú had spoken so much (Garrigú! Garrigú...! hmm...!) stretched out on a bed of fennel, with its scales still pearly, as if they had recently come out of the waves, and with a bouquet of fragrant herbs in their monster noses. And the vision of all these wonders was so vivid that Don Balaguer thought for a moment that those succulent dishes were already served on the embroidered tablecloth of the altar, and two or three times, instead of the Dominus vobiscum, said the Benedict. But leaving aside these slight mistakes, the poor father officiated according to his duties, without jumping a line or omitting a genuflection. Everything was so until the conclusion of the first Mass.

–And there goes one! –said the chaplain with a sigh of relief. Incontinent, without wasting a minute, beckoned the sacristan, or rather, the one he thought was his sacristan, to call for the second mass.

And here begins the second Mass and with it the sin of Don Balaguer. "Faster, quicker, quicker", says Garrigú's diabolical bell with a squeaky and sour voice, and this time the officiant abandons himself to the domain of gluttony, devours the pages of the Missal, with the greed of his over-excited appetite. He frenetically kneels, rises, sketches the figure of the cross, hastens all his gestures, all his movements to finish sooner. He barely hits his chest with the Confiteor, when he extends his arms in the Gospel. Between him and the sacristan there is a diabolical race. Verses and answers rush, they run over. Words pronounced half-heartedly, without opening their mouths, because this would have required a useless waste of time, end in incomprehensible syllables.

Like rushed grape harvesters, who bruise the grapes in the barrels, both spoil the Latin of the mass, blowing off unbroken splinters of the language. And during this frightening vertigo, the infernal bell, always ringing, spurs the wretched chaplain, like those bells that are hung on horses to make them jog tickling.

Imagine in what brief moments the mass would end!

–And that's two! –the reverend muttered, panting. But without allowing time to breathe, his face lit, sweating from the frightened forehead, he comes down trembling in the steps of the altar and...

Behold, the third Mass begins

A few minutes more, and the dining room will be finally uncovered before his eyes. But, alas, as dinner approaches, the unhappy Don Balaguer feels more and more moved by the mad impatience of the gluttony. The golden carps, the roasted young goats are there; he touches them, he touches them... The platters smoke, the wines embalm, and, shaking its stinging rattle, the bell says without rest: –faster!, faster!, faster!

But how could he go any faster? His lips barely move; he no longer pronounces words. From temptation to temptation, he began by jumping one verse and now he jumps two. The Epistle is too long and does not end it. He stutters the first words of the Gospel. He suppresses the Lord's Prayer and salutes the Preface from afar. And so, with leaps and jumps, he rushes into the sin spurred on by Garrigú; "Vade retro, Satan!", who seconds him with prodigious insight, lifting the chasuble, turning the leaves of the missal two by two and four by four, pouring out the cruets and chirping demoniacally more and more quickly.

It was to see the frightened face of the assistants! Forced to follow, guided by the mime of the father, that mass, of which they did not understand a word, they stood up when the others knelt, and in all the phases of that office never seen before, the crowd turned in the pews with different attitudes. The Christmas star, which was advancing through the sky, on its way to the little stable, paled with fright and terror.

–The father prays too quickly! –The Marquise said without stopping, shaking her clean, white coat. The mayor, with the steel glasses riding on his nose, searches uselessly in his devotional for the passage that the priest prays. But, strictly speaking, those good people, to whom the hope of the supper stings, are not angry because of the precipitation of the Mass, and when Don Balaguer, with his face shining, turns to the auditorium and exclaims with all his strength: *Ite, missa est,* the chorus with one voice says: *Deogratias,* with such a clean accent, so cheerful, that it seems mixed and confused with the first toasts of the supper.

Five minutes later, that crowd of gentlemen entered the great hall and took a seat around the table, presided over by the chaplain. The castle, illuminated from top to bottom, was filled with songs and laughter and rumors, and the venerable Balaguer plunged his fork into a capon wing, drowning his remorse with the Pope's wine and the healthy juice of meat. So much did the blessed father eat and drink, that he died that night of a tremendous stroke, without time to repent, and in the morning he reached the heavens, still echoing the songs of the feast.

–Go away, you bad Christian! –they said to him. Your fault is enough great to erase a whole life of virtue. You sinned by saying an unworthy Christmas Mass. Well then, in payment, you will not be able to enter Heaven until after saying three hundred Christmas Masses, in the presence of all those who sinned with you!

Here is the true legend of don Balaguer, as it is told in the land of olive trees. Now, the castle of Trinquelag no longer exists, but the chapel is still preserved, erect and straight, among the bouquet of green oaks that crown the mountain. The wind blows and beats the disjointed door; the grass gets in the way of the ground; there are nests in the corners of the altar and in the openings of the windows whose glasses have long since disappeared. However, it is said that every year, on Christmas Eve, a supernatural light wanders through the ruins; and that, on the way to the church, the peasants contemplate that spectral chapel, illuminated by invisible candles that burn outdoors, between the winds and the snow. Smile, if it pleases you; but a grape harvester of the region affirms that one Christmas night, being in the mountain, lost in the vicinity of the ruins, he saw... raises the hair what he saw. Until eleven o'clock, nothing. Everything was silent, motionless and dull. But when midnight rang, a bell, perhaps forgotten in the ruined bell tower, an old bell, now out of date, which seemed to ring fifteen leagues away, rang mass. Then, down the slope of the road, the unhappy late-nighter saw indecisive shadows waving and opaque flashlights rising. Already near the ruins, voices from invisible throats murmured:

–Good night, Mr. Mayor.

–Good night, good night, my children.

When the group of ghosts entered the chapel, the poor grape harvester, who is brave, approached the door on tiptoe, and seeing through the broken wood, he witnessed a rare spectacle. All the ghosts he had seen pass were lined up around the choir and in the ruined ship, as if there were still benches and armchairs. And among them were great ladies clothed in brocade, with their lace hoods; knights full of embroidery, and workers in floral jackets, such as they must have been worn in the remote days of our grandparents; all of them looking decrepit, yellow, dusty and fatigued. At every moment, the owls, guests of the chapel, awakened by the light, made their rounds around the candles, whose flame rose vague and erect as if burning inside a gauze. And it was a matter of seeing a character, whose nose was ridden with steel glasses, moving at every moment his black wig, on which an owl had stood, beating its enormous wings in silence.

There in the background, an old man of very short stature, put in the middle of the choir, waved a bell without a clapper that no longer produced any sound, while standing next to the altar, clad in a chasuble whose gold was already greenish, a priest whose voice did not produce any rumor at all seemed to say mass. It was Don Balaguer saying his third mass!

The Suicides

Today it is fashionable to raise the lid of coffins, open or break the doors of other people's houses, put your hand in the pocket of a secret, like the thief in the pocket of the clock, be a secular confessor of the whole world and violate the secrecy of confession, take publicly and as honor the profession of spy and informer, in short, to be an indiscreet reporter, no one will take it badly that I publish, silencing the signatory's name because of a candid excess of modesty, because of archaism, the letter of a suicidal man, who in no way resembled the unfortunates of whom the press has spoken lately.

***

A few nights ago, in the harlequin gazette of a newspaper, I read the news of a recent suicide. The paragraph about the unfortunate event shamelessly jingles the buffoon's bells; it refers to that suicide with the flirtatious and playful pen that was used shortly before to refer to a scandalous dinner or a gallant adventure of the court; it speaks of death with the same grace that it would use to describe, in the chronicle of a dance, the white suit of Mrs. X. It is about a young man who, on the first day of his journey, prostrates himself with fatigue and throws with disdain the knotty staff that has served him; about a mother who cries without consolation, looking at the still lukewarm space her son occupied at her home; and all this is referred to simply and cheerfully, with a smile on the lips, savoring the thin cigarette that has been lit when leaving the theater. This nervous laughter, which is not that of Lucretius when he mocks with wrath his ancient gods; which is not that of Lord Byron when he feels his spirit surrounded by the strong rings of the vipers that devoured the body of Laocoon; which is not Gilbert's as he approaches the tomb, surrounded by roses; which cannot be compared to any of this, because it is not engendered by pain, doubt or skepticism, it seemed to me to be the laughter of an imbecile before the pit full of corpses. And taking the printed page out of my sight, I remembered with repugnance Boccaccio's Decameron, appearing in the days of the plague of Florence.

The epidemic that now devours us is even more terrible than the one that decimated the unhappy Florentines when Boccaccio's shameless book was published. Suicide is no longer an isolated fact: it is no longer a plague. I don't know what strange concatenation, what mysterious complicity links these crimes; but they don't come alone, one follows the other, they reach each other as if suicide were a contagious disease, like fever. We should find out which is the Ganges which produces these poisonous miasmas. In Hamlet's monologue, which is a precious fact about the idea of suicide in the 16th century, the terrors of doubt are clearly perceived. Today, as the doors of eternity open, no one wonders what the dream of the tomb might be. One dies with a smile on his lips, tasting the romantic and syrupy gazettes in which the public will be made aware of the event. Our modern Hamlet, after a succulent lunch, does not formulate the *to be or not to be*; he takes the poison, and, if he is frank, if he is sincere, he writes a letter to a friend, like this one that I keep in the most secret drawer of my law firm:

"Gentleman: I am going to kill myself because I do not have a single coin in my pocket, nor a single illusion in my head. The man is nothing more than a sack of meat to be filled with money. When the sack is empty, it is useless.

A long time ago, when I was fifteen years old, when I was trembling at the sound of lightning, I believed in God. My mother was still alive, and in the evenings before going to bed, she made me kneel on my bed and pray to the Virgin. Forgive me if the previous lines are almost erased: when I think of my mother, tears come to my eyes.

I still seem to be watching the ceremony of my first communion. Many days before, I had been preparing myself for this solemn act. At night I would go to the cell of an old priest who indoctrinated me. How puerile fears used to assault my poor thought in those nights! I can assure you that my conscience was then a white page, and yet the idea of communion in sin terrified me. As I went out through the silent cloister, only illuminated from time to time by one or other agonizing bulb, walking on tiptoe so as not to hear the echo of my footsteps, it seemed to me that the giant forms of prelates and monks, detached from the enormous canvases of the wall, were going to chase me, dragging their robes and cassocks heavily. One night –the night I confessed– all those delusions of a sick imagination disappeared; I left the cell rejoicing as if carrying the sky within my spirit. There were the prelates with their mitres, and the monks, girded, hooded, motionless and mute in the colossal paintings of the great cloister; but instead of chasing me with a grim frown, they smiled at my step affectionately. What a soft night that was! At dawn of the following day I came to imagine that the bells rang the dawn inside my chest. It seems impossible, gentleman, that a superstition and a lie can make men happy.

Today I am ten thousand leagues away from that day. During this dark parenthesis, I have devoted myself with determination and zeal to study the great Book of Science. Like a lady after the dance, in the mystery of her boudoir illuminated by the discreet light of a rosy candlelight, strips herself of her adornments and jewels, and so I stripped myself of the simple beliefs of my childhood. In each book, like the sheep in each bush, I have been leaving, torn, the fleece of faith. And the winter of life is so sad when there is not a single belief that covers us! Illusions are the cloak of old age.

As long as I believed in God I was happy. I endured life, because life is the way of death. After these hardships –I told myself–, there is a heaven in which one rests. The tomb is a palm in the middle of the desert. Every suffering, every anguish, every anguish is a step on that mysterious ladder seen by Jacob and which takes us to heaven. On the way to Tabor, one may well pass through Calvary. But imagine Columbus' rage if, after having ventured into the unknown sea, nature had told him: America does not exist! Imagine my rage, when after accepting suffering, because this is the way to heaven, I knew with horror that heaven was a lie. Oh, I remembered then John Paul Rhichter! The cemetery was covered with shadows; tombs yawned and wandering spirits made their way; only children slept in their marble tombs. There was the quadrant of eternity, with no needles, no numbers, nothing but a black hand that rotated and rotated eternally. A white Christ with the pale whiteness of sadness arose in the tabernacle. Is there a God? –the dead asked. And Christ answered:

No, the heavens are empty; in the depths of the earth only the drop of rain is heard, falling like an eternal tear. And the children awoke, and lifting up their little hands, they exclaimed, Jesus, Jesus, do we no longer have a father? And Christ, closing his bloodless arms, exclaimed sternly:

–Sons of the century: you and I are all orphans!

To this terrible voice that rolled down through the crowded masses of shadows, the tombs were closed with a crash, the candles were suddenly extinguished and the terrible night spread its crow's wing over the world.

Children of the century, we are all orphans! How many times, gentleman, I have repeated these words in my hours of anguish! We are all orphans! My soul is numb, and needs, to keep moving, the warmth of a belief!

But I have squandered my wealth of faith, and in the bottom of my heart there is not a single eighth of hope left. I am an empty pocket and a conscience without faith. When the sack is useless, it breaks. That's what I do".

Story of a chorus girl

OVERDUE LETTER

For the edification of the enthusiast dandies who receive with laurels and palms the choristers imported by Mauricio Grau, I copy a letter that belongs to my secret archive and that –if memory is not unfaithful to me– I received, soon a year ago, on the same day that the French troupe deserted from our theater.

The letter reads as follows:

"My little blue pig:

With my foot on the foot-board of the wagon and the best of my beauty in my suitcase, I write some lines in the yellowish light of a candle, made on purpose by some distraught merchant to discredit the factory of the Star. My companion snores in her iron cot, and I, sitting in a drawer, where the only remains of my wardrobe are going to be immersed very soon, I am entertained in drawing scribbles and lines like your journalists, men who, for lack of champagne and Burgundy, drink to large sips that thick and dark liquid called ink. The show has just ended, and I have a large part of the night at my disposal. I, accustomed to squandering other people's capital, waste nights and days, which do not belong to me either: they belong to time.

If I had had the good fortune of M. Perret, my companion; if luck, that crazy woman, crazier than us, had sent me in the form of a lottery ticket two thousand pesos, ten thousand francs, I would not have taken the pen to write my confessions. Men write when they don't have money, and women when they want to ask for something.

For want of any other entertainment, let's talk about my life. I am going to satisfy your curiosity, to stop seeing you on tiptoe, looking at the window of my intimate life. The woman who, like me, has the cynicism to appear on the stage in the economic suit of Paradise, can perfectly write her biography without scruples.

I don't know where I was born. I presume that my parents, whose memory was a little skinny, no longer remembered me a few weeks after my birth. All my memories begin in the smoky cubicle where I passed my first years, in the company of a worn-out, 60-year-old woman, who worked as an usher in a small Parisian theater. Why did that good woman pick me up? I could never know, although I suspect that this good deed had little to do with charity. I took care of the kitchen and invariably did as many patches as were necessary in the frayed wardrobe of my protector. A few pinches and a few slaps were the reward for my daily efforts. We ate badly and slept worse, because, if the show ended after midnight, I punctually waited for the return of the usher, instead I had to stand as soon as the dawn came, to prepare, as well as I could, the poor lunch and to fulfill, the venerable necessities of the house.

I rarely went to the show. My protector feared, rightly, that dealing with the people of the theater would ruin my customs. But as I grew, my ambitions also grew. The hovel in which we lived stifled my instincts for independence and joy. A young lighting technician, who lived behind the wall or our attic, had told me that I was pretty. I turned ten years old, twelve years old, fifteen years old, and a happy September morning, I carefully packed a suitcase, I put in it the loud rags with which I used to dress on feast days, and, without waiting for the return of Madame Ulysses, since there was nothing else to take, I took the door.

Suspensive points.

If you have Ariadne's thread, follow me as you can in the great Parisian labyrinth. If you do not have it, or you aren't skillful enough to navigate along the reefs, be content to follow me from afar, when I appear again at the surface of the earth. Victor Hugo has said:

> *"In the brambles of life, each one*
> *leaves one thing behind: the sheep*
> *his white wool, man his virtue."*

Where it says man put woman: it is a simple errata correction.

Here I am again, less poor, after my subterranean excursions. The doors of a theater open to my growing beauty, and the sky of the backstage covers with its rags my foolishness. The businessman was a gouty man, sick and dirty, who paid perfectly badly the unfortunate debutants. With what I earned in that theater I could buy three pairs of boots and a few boxes of matches. But this was a completely secondary matter. I never aspired to live, as an artist, from the theater. I could barely read; my great musical knowledge would have attracted a downpour of boiled potatoes over my head. Either art wasn't made for me, or I wasn't born for art. The only thing I was looking for in the theater was as a permanent exhibition, well placed in an aristocratic sideboard. When a woman resolves to turn her beauty into a stock business, the best market is a theater.

Those who don't know anything about the backstage, figure that the door of that Garden of the Hesperides is very well guarded by fabulous dragons and monsters. In that paradise... of Muhammad, of course, unlike any other paradise, the entrance is free for sinners.

I, however, lost like an atom in the rose-colored mass of the choirs, lived painfully, coddled by misery and victim of deprivation.

My magnificent and extraordinary beauty, according the poor lighting technician, my ex-neighbor, passed unnoticed in that theater, as the piece of satin, blue or white, also passes unnoticed in the great store full of lace, silk and gold fabrics. The competition was fearsome. Like Marlborough's wife from the top of her tower, I expected not the return, but the appearance of someone I did not yet know.

But, alas, no Russian prince, no English lord came into sight in that long season. I suppose that Russian princes are imaginary entities that have only existed in the hollow brains of novelists. Money was moving away from me, like swallows when winter arrives and friends when poverty arrives.

My old protector remembered me. She made me advantageous propositions, and, seduced by her great promises, I came to America, the land of gold. The Yankees, who know admirably all the goods, except for the woman, took me for a real Parisian. In New York, there is dinner.

There are red and blood faces worth ten million, and frightful buttoned frock coats that hold a fortune in the wallet. I don't speak English, but they speak gold. To answer them, just one word from the vocabulary would suffice:

Yes.

Americans are the only men who speak money.

Havana is a privileged country. It's very hot. The blacks serve to highlight the hyperborean whiteness of the European women.

There are men who, by force of living among sugar loaves, get used to crumble their fortune like a lump placed in water. But Havana is the country of sugar and New York is the country of gold. Don't talk to me about races or figures: there are no more gallant men than the Yankees.

My impressions of the trip come to an end. We were already in Mexico. I had been told that this was the land of spring. I, however, have seen it only in the exuberant corset of the Leroux and in the bouquets that the conductor buys every night. I expected to see golden sands running through the streets, as they did among the waves of the Pactolo; unfortunately, I have found nothing but complaisant journalists, friends who usually have dinner from time to time, and elegant dandies who treat us as if we were ladies of the *Faubourg Saint Germain*. It is a simple mistake: *Notre Dâme de Lorette* is farther away.

Every night I look at myself courted behind the scenes by a mob of stylish men and young men who talk to me with their heads uncovered, scrupulously pulling the cigar so as not to bother me with the smoke. And they all dispute my smiles; they send me a thousand flowers that transcend the Rambouillet Hotel and –the height of folly!– they even write me letters. The most audacious of them usually invite me to drink a redcurrant or champagne... vermouth. They find me in the streets, and, turning aside politely to give me the sidewalk, they take off their hats. Some revelers have kissed my hand.

There are no Russian princes here either. But on the other hand, I carry a complete collection of autographs, which are more precious. This is the first city where I am treated like a lady. You'll see if I have reason to be grateful".

In the street

Down the street, by one of those neighborhoods that the carriages cross on their way to Peralvillo, there is a poor house, without sun curtains on the balconies or lace curtains on the stained glass windows, washed away and eaten by the raining waters, that stripped the paint from its white walls, twisted the gutters with their weight, and even filled the cornice of the windows with fungus and mold. I, who pass little or nothing through those neighborhoods, fixed my gaze with curiosity on each of its features and details. The carriage in which I was going was moving slowly, and as we advanced, I was seriously saddened. Whenever I leave for Peralvillo it seems to me that I am going to be buried. Distracted, I fixed my eyes on the balcony of the little house I have described. A blessed palm crossed between the bars of the handrail and, doing curtain work, climbed the wall and a modest creeper curdled with green leaves and blue bells was twisted on the iron rod. At the bottom, in a porcelain pot, stood the green, round and well combed head of basil. All that breathed poverty, clean poverty; everything seemed to be beautifully arranged by gloveless hands, but washed with almond soap. I looked inside, and near the balcony, sitting in a large wheelchair, between two white cushions, her brief feet on a small stool, there was a woman, almost a girl, skinny, pale, with a transparent complexion like the thin leaves of Chinese porcelain, black eyes, deeply black, circled by the sad violets of insomnia. It was enough to see her to understand that she was dying of tuberculosis. Her hands looked like wax; she breathed with sorrow, laboriously, leaning her head, which no longer had the strength to stand upright, on the pillow that served as her backrest, and seeing with her eyes, enlarged by fever, that showy crowd that walked in a festive manner to the races, waving the satin umbrella or the ivory fan, the Indian cane or the cherry tree. The carriages passed with the harmonious noise of its new springs; the landau, opening its gondola, lined with satin blue, discovered the resplendent silk of the costumes and the whiteness of the epidermis of its passengers; the phaeton was jumping like a fugitive deer, and the mail coach, crowned with white hats and red umbrellas, with the ladies flirtatiously stepped on the coachman's seat and on the roof, was running heavily, like an old bachelor in love, behind the grizzly eyes. And it seemed that voices came out of the stones, that a vague noise of celebration was formed in the airs, confusing the argentinean laughter of the young people, the spraying of the cars on the pavement, the cracking of the whip that twists like a viper in the airs, the confused sound of the words and the trot of the fatigued horses. This is it: life that passes, swirls, bubbles, boils; mouths that smile, eyes that kiss with the look, feathers, silks, white lace and black eyelashes; the rumor of the party shelling its necklace of sonorous pearls in the greenish glasses of that humble house, where a young existence was being extinguished and two black pupils were being extinguished, as a candle is extinguished licking with its flame the washer, and as the white lights of the dawn fade and extinguish. The sun seems to redden the silk of the umbrellas and the blood of the veins: maybe you won't see her tomorrow, poor girl! All that crowd sings, laughs: you no longer have the strength to cry, and you see that changeable panorama, as the soul that was struggling in the drafts of a lock would see the curves and arabesques of dance. You are already moving away from life, like a white mist that the morning sun does not heat. Others will display their beauty in the cushions of the carriage, in the tribunes of the turf, and in the boxes of the theater; they will dress you in white, they will put the yellow palm between your hands, and the oscillating flame of the yellow candles will lose its reflections in the rigid folds of your suit and in the white orange blossoms, adornment of your black hair.

You cling to life, as the sick little boy clings to the bars of his bed, so that he will not be thrown into the tub filled with cold water. You, poor child, have hardly lived. What do you know about the parties in which the glass of the thin glasses crashes and loving words are murmured? You have lived alone and poor, like the red flower that grows in the granular hollow of an old wall or in the canyon of a crooked canal. However, you do not envy those who pass by. You no longer have the strength to desire!

Looking away from that picture, I fixed my gaze on the passing carriages.

The landau in which Cecilia was on her way to the races had the shape of a gondola, with a dark blue varnish and a white lining. The big casings of the wheels shone as if they were made of gold, and the spokes, new and lustrous, rotated dazzling the glances with reflections of new varnish. It was grim to think that those wheels were touching the angular pebbles, the hard stones and the muddy sand of the avenues. Cecilia reclined on the fluffy cushions, with the gloating and delight of a woman who, before feeling the contact of silk, felt the scratches of sackcloth. She was happy; she was known to have just eaten truffles. If a bird had committed the clumsiness of confusing his lips with the branches of myrtle, he would have sipped the last drop of champagne in that scarlet amphora.

Cecilia squinted her eyelids so as not to feel the crude reverberation of the sun. The red umbrella threw on her picaresque face and her lilac dress a fire reflection. The rump of the horses, wounded by the light, looked like Florentine bronze. The curious, when they saw her, asked:

–Who would she be?

And a philosopher friend, remembering a certain graphic phrase, said:

–A duchess or a prostitute.

Only the sick and dying woman knew this woman. She was his sister.

By the fireside

You are going to doubt it; but by God and my soul I protest that I speak very truthfully, formally. And after all, why shouldn't you believe that I live cheerfully, very cheerfully in winter? I see how one by one the already yellow leaves of the trees fall; I hear their monotonous clicking as I cross some silent avenue on my evening walks; my face is whipped by the breath of December, like the thin, penetrating blade of a Toledo dagger, and far from sheltering myself at the bottom of a carriage, far from renouncing those evening runs, I say to myself: Hail, winter! Blessed are you who arrive with the deep blue of your sky and the calm and silence of your nights! Blessed are you who bring the long and tasty talks with which the good old man entertains the evenings at home, while the chestnuts jump in the fire and the freezing blasts whip the tallest trees of the park!

Hail, winter! I have no park in which the wind can whisper, nor do I spend the evenings by the loving fire of the home; but I salute you, and delight myself thinking of those family parties, when I walk the streets and squares, saying, like the good Campoamor, when I see through the cracks of the doors the sparkling home of a friend:

Those who sleep there are not cold.

The cold! Give me something more imaginary than this decanted character. I only believe in the cold when I see those unhappy people crossing the streets and squares who, without any more shelter than their humble summer coat, their heads covered by a shameful hat, shivering, and a step away from freezing, seem to be saying like the philosopher Bias:

Omnia mecum porto[1].

Poor children, not having a coat in winter is like not having a belief in old age!

I have always believed that fire is the least warming thing in the ice season. Try singing.

I know a bachelor, a man in his fifties, rich as Rothschild, selfish as Diogenes and a gourmet as Lord Palbroke. He is rich; he has a superb house; ten perfectly comfortable carriages; a splendid servitude and a table that would honor Luculus. No one, seeing him lying on the docks on the cushions of his comfortable sedan, pulled by two american horses, covered by a hefty overcoat against which nothing could the ice of Siberia itself; no one, I say, could think that he is unfortunate, perfectly unfortunate; that this superb Creso suffers from a terrible disease: the cold!

Our man, our banker, our millionaire, is cold. And it is the worst thing that neither the Norwegian chimney, nor the Asian skins that he has in his palace, are enough to fight that eternal snow. He locks himself in his house; he looks for the soft heat of the stoves; he shelters his numb limbs with the skins brought by him from St. Petersburg; with the thick doors and the long curtains he prevents some gusts of wind from penetrating easily through the joints; he believes himself to be safe, he sinks into the cushions of a winter canapé; but he is alone, entirely alone; There is not a single hand that wipes away his tears, if he cries; if he dies, no one will come to comfort him in his agony, no one will go to pray in his grave: Youth? It's over! Love? Impossible! Riches? What are they worth? Remembrance? It's remorse! Death? Death? The logs of the chimney creak as if they were also crying; the crystals tremble; the rooms are deserted and gloomy... What loneliness! what sadness! what a horrible cold!

My good friend:

I know that you love me and that's why I'm writing to you to steal some moment from the holy happiness of my existence. I'm so happy! Remember my Lupe? She's so good, so simple! I love her carelessly, as you say! It's so beautiful the little angel that God has given us! If you could see it! Her head is blond and her eyes are bright, wet, like his mother's. Soul of my soul! When I see her asleep in her cradle, with her hands folded on her chest; when I warm her numb little feet with my kisses, it seems to me that there is no happiness... It cannot be! Like mine, and I cry, yes, I'm not ashamed to say it, I cry like a simpleton, I hug Lupe, my other angel, and I jump like a child... Let's go! I think I'm going to go crazy with joy!

Come with us; we are waiting for you. Leave your monotonous strolls, the coffee shops, the dances, the theaters; come and forget your eternal ill-

---

1 All that is mine I carry with me.

humor. You will see how you envy me... Yes, because envy is sometimes very just and even holy. Look: we'll arrange your bedroom in a piece uphol- stered in blue, as you like it; you'll find some flower pots in the window; a comfortable and fluffy armchair next to the warm bed, and on the bedside table some books, like Monsieur, Madame et Bebé.

You'll see if I'm lucky, when on these long winter nights I return early to my little house, and while Lupe, with her white robe and her rose, white too, in her hair, touches some of those waltzes that tickle your feet, I lazily read some good book, looking at my wife from the corner of my eye, which is a book certainly more worthy to be read, than all the books that you gather in your library.

We are not rich: you well know it; but when after working during the day I return to my home, and Lupe, with our angel in her arms, comes out to receive me, I am so happy, I judge myself so happy that... What riches are there that can be compared to the holy peace of my soul? If you are sad, if you are disappointed, come and spend a few days with us: we are so happy, that we would like to go out into those streets saying it with a loud voice, so that all would participate in our happiness!

CARLOS

You see, lady or miss; my friend Carlos, without stoves, coats or floats, enjoys a warmth that is not enjoyed by the most famous millionaire. The soul! Here is the chimney that must be well provided for the long nights of winter.

> *Because winter is not about kissing and cold,*
> *And the deserted roads we saw yesterday;*
> *It is the heart without light, it is the soul without greenery,*
> *That's what I'll be when you're no longer there!*

I have for me that the memory is a heater that must be really thought of, when the industrial furor, ever-growing, depletes the charcoal mines. I know that I find in the arsenal of my memory, the snows and the ice of the poles, as well as the fire of Africa and Asia. That's why when I sink my head in the hot pillow, I wrap myself with the bedspreads and wait for the soft caresses of the dream, while I watch how it decomposes and transforms the smoke that ascends in spiral of my cigarette, I evoke, if I experience a convulsion of cold, some memory and I warm myself to its fantastic shade. Do you doubt it?

I have a friend already advanced in years, but young in spirit; a poet, if there are any, although in his life –and be careful since it is long– he has had the idea of threading a verse; father of two strong young men, with mus- taches and sturdy as two sergeants; and at the end, as dessert, also a merchant. It is, however, that neither the snow of numbers, nor the eagerness of practical life, have been enough to annihilate the poetic enthusiasm of my friend, who still, under the frost of gray hair, feels the generous bonfire of youth boil. A few nights ago, the two of us departed amicably, both sitting around a papier maché table, loaded with many signs, with two Chinese cups of transparent porcelain, a superb coffee maker full of tasty moka, and an open box of covetous tobaccos, still fresh from the humid sea breezes. We were talking about the cold, and my friend, with his cascading voice, told me, if my memory is not unfaithful, the following:

–In my youth I had a bride, as beautiful as a figure from Ticiano, as blond as the ears of wheat, and so simple that, had I not told her, she would not have known, but God knows, that she was beautiful. Poor Clara! She loved me like a woman loves when she is fifteen. I loved her with all the fire of my twenties, and even when I remember it, it seems to me that I still love her! One afternoon we went out, as usual, through the countryside; she leaned on my arm; I was confused and trembling like a child waiting for the sentence of some innocent sin. Without feeling it, she and I moved away from those who came behind, little by little getting into the most intricate part of the foliage. I felt her arm trembling next to mine, I saw how modesty dyed her countenance with a pink dye... Suddenly, Clara detaches from my arm, and throwing a loud laugh, she runs like a hawk through the field; I follow her, I already catch up with her; she stretches her arms, narrows her waist; she turns her face, I look at a small cluster of grapes between her lips, I want to take it away from her, she defends herself, and without wanting to, almost without thinking about it, our lips unite, and a kiss the holiest, the purest, the most sublime, suddenly sounds between that solitude and that silence.

Do you tell me if these memories do not produce an affectionate warmth?

Winter, winter! They say you are a portrait of old age! Today you are then the portrait of humanity: we are all old!

Smoke-colored Stories

Juan the organist

I

The Rambla valley, unknown to many geographers who don't have a clue, is, without dispute, one of the most fertile, extensive and cheerful in which the spirit can be refreshed, soar and expand. It is not very near or very far: behind those mountains that climb its blue crest in the distance, not far from the volcanoes, whose perpetual snow bites the sun when it breaks them; there it is. In times not even remote, stagecoaches and carriages of every type, some driven by mules, horsemen, groups of animals of burden, muleteers and humble Indians, dirty and barefoot, crossed that valley daily. Today the railroad, giving a different channel to the traffic of merchandise and to the current of travelers, has isolated and subdued the fertile valley. The towns, once visited by travelers of all kinds and colors, are unfrequented, poor, but still are proud and haughty, like the rich who come to less. Remains of the former prominence only remain in the mute streets, very old and unwashed, whose courtyards, stables, corrals and other wide outbuildings clearly indicate that they once served as staging posts or inns.

In the current years, the valley of the Rambla does not experience any more movement than that of tillage. Several farms dispute their possession: one here, another there; this one is sheltered and huddled at the foot of the mountain; that other one goes down to the river in a graceful curve, and all of them, from the courtly and presumptuous one, that reaching the gates of the population wants to enter there, to the sullen and hermit that climbs the mountain with its brown houses, looking for the thickness of cedars, whether in erected ears, whether in dense and undulating cornfields, in robust breeding or in rich woods, pay abundant tribute each year. Nothing more fertile or more joyful than that valley, now seen when it begins to clear, now in the afternoon nap or in the solemn moment of twilight. The snow of volcanoes, like sea water, changes its tints according to the point where the sun is; it either appears pink, or with a hyperborean dazzling whiteness, or purple. Many times the clouds, like the cadenced curtain of a great thalamus, prevent us from seeing the white woman and the smoking mountain. It is necessary for the light, serving as an obedient waitress, to open the humid gauze pavilion so that we can see the colossal companions. "The white woman" then blushes as a newlywed whom some importunate surprises on the bed. It would be said that she lifts the sheets and the bedspreads with the morbid knee. Not so at the end of the afternoon: the white woman looks like a lying statue at such hours:

> *Tired of combat*
> *In that lively fight,*
> *Sometimes I remember with envy*
> *That dark, hidden corner.*
> *Of that mute and pale*
> *Woman, I remember and say:*
> *Oh, what a silent love of death!*
> *What a dream of a quiet sepulchre!*

The sown fields display all the shades of green, forming in the graduations of color, by the contrast with the blond of the harvest, by the lines and clippings of the cornfield, like a board of colossal dimensions and picturesque simplicity. The trees do not cut off the view; they flee from the valley and retreat to the mountains. They are the old and penitent hermits who move away from the world. What we can see by far are the single-door houses where the workers live; the barns with their oblong skylights, the still water of the dams, the old gates of each farm and the towers of churches and chapels. Every village, however insignificant and poor it may be, has its own temple. You will certainly not find in these pious factories the sophistication of art: the bell towers are small, chubby; each temple seems to be saying to the natives: "I too am barefoot and naked like you". But on the other hand, nothing is as cheerful as the clamor of those small bells on Sunday mornings, or on the eve of a feast. There the bells ring differently than in the city: they ring to glory.

The animated part of the landscape can be painted with a few strokes: Do you see that flock grazing; those oxen pulling the plough; that laborer who, sitting on the ground, takes his omelettes with chili sauce, in the meantime the woman drinks from a jar with fermented cactus juice; the child, almost naked, who crosses by the door of his hut, the woman with her sagging breasts, leaning over the grinding stone, and the master, covered by the wide wings of a palm hat, riding his horse over the sown fields? Well, they are the only figures in the landscape. In the first hours of the morning and the last hours of the afternoon also appear, with wide brimmed straw hats and long riding suits, in better-looking horses, harnessed with more style, the "girls" of the hacienda. Also when it gets dark you can see the chaplain, who always carries the prayer book in one hand and the umbrella open in the other to get rid of the sun, rain or night dew.

And with these figures, the carts loaded with harvest, the gold dust that surrounds the threshing floor like a mystical halo, the vigilant mastiffs, the roar of the bulls, the bleating of the sheep, the neighing of the horses and the monotonous song with which the workers accompany their work, you can form in the imagination a picture that I cannot describe. First of all, stretch out over the valley a very blue and transparent sky, a sky in which one does not see God but the Virgin; a sky whose clouds, when it has them, seem to be made with dove's feathers that the wind has been stealing little by little; a sky that resembles the eyes of my first bride and the smooth petals of the forget-me-not.

II

Juan the organist arrived at one of the ranches of that valley, some day, after dark. He was thirty years old and had a regular figure, expressive eyes, a clean suit, although poor, and fine manners. I know little about his history: I am told that he was born in a good cradle and that his father held some important jobs during the time of President Herrera. Juan did not experienced more than the last gasps of the paternal fortune, consumed in unhappy businesses. However, with or without sacrifice, his parents gave him an excellent education. Juan knew how to play the piano and the organ; he painted moderately well; he knew grammar, mathematics, geography, history, some natural sciences and two languages: French and Latin. With this knowledge and these skills he was able to earn his living as a teacher and contribute to the subsistence of his parents. They died in the same month, precisely when Mexico was under siege. Juan, who was a good son, cried for them, and seeing himself alone and without relatives, submitting to practical needs, conceived the firm intention of getting married as soon he could, by finding a good woman, industrious, poor like him and who would please him. It did not take him long to find what he looked for. Perhaps the girl who he had noticed did not meet all the conditions and attributes expressed above, but in matters of love, the poor are easy to please, especially if they have certain poetic hobbies and have read novels. To the love they feel, they add the gratitude inspired by a woman sufficiently detached from worldly vanities and pomp, to say to them: "I love you". They think they achieved a real coup, they admire their good fortune, they praise God who gives them so much joy, and they close their eyes with which they should examine the defects of the bride, to see only her virtues and excellences. The poor receive everything as alms: even affection.

Juan set his eyes on a fairly beautiful and prudent girl, poor in condition, but well admitted, by the background of her family, in the best houses. She was the daughter of a colonel who married a rich woman and threw her fortune away in a few years. The widow was left without widowhood, because the colonel served the Empire. But as her sisters, brothers and relatives lived in a good position, she never lacked enough to pay the rent of the house (twenty-five pesos), the food (fifty) or the other small expenses of absolute and indispensable necessity. In order to dress the girls well, as well as people of the class they were, she had his troubles at first; but they, after they entered in age, knew how to turn the old dress of a cousin into a fashionable dress and to make the most prodigious metamorphoses with all kinds of fabrics and ribbons. In addition, they were pretty and discreet; they won the will of their relatives, giving them sweets and trinkets made by them; so that they never lacked the garments that enhance the beauty of the ladies and not only dressed with decorum and good taste, but with a certain luxury and elegance. Every day of a saint's day, or when the traditional solemnities such as Easter and the Day of the Dead were approaching, they received dresses, hats, a box of gloves or a case of perfumes. There came a time when it was no longer necessary for them to resort to the turns, arrangements or patches in which they so much exceeded, and they even gave to other girls, poorer than themselves, the leftovers of their wardrobe. The other rich girls pampered them very much and used to take them on walks and to theaters.

Rosa was the one who married Juan. The other three, however ambitious or less fortunate, remained single. There was no lack of one who, knowing the marriage, made sad predictions. "Juan", they said, "earns his living by working; today he earns one hundred and fifty pesos every month; but what are these for Rosa's aspirations, accustomed to the ease and luxury with which her relatives and friends live?". And indeed, it was even strange and surprising that Rosa would have corresponded to the poor boy love. The fact is that, whether it was because she wanted to get married, or because she truly loved Juan, Rosa accepted the mediocre, for no saying worse, condition that the suitor offered her, and she got married.

The first year they were quite happy; it is true that they had their arguments and dislikes; that Rosa sighed when she heard the noise of the carriages that were heading for the promenade; that she didn't go to the theater because her husband didn't want her to go to someone else's box, but with mutual disappointments and suffocated desires, making unprecedented efforts to polish the husband's one hundred and fifty pesos, the first nine months passed.

The discomfort and disruption of the treasury in the last days of Lerdo coincided with the birth of the girl that God sent them. The salary of Juan was not paid, it was necessary to appeal to friends, to moneylenders, to pawn things, and Rosa, in such critical circumstances, confessed to herself that she had made a great mistake marrying poor Juan, when she could, as another friend of hers, catch a wealthy husband. The conjugal storms were then most terrible. The girl's graces and beauties did not flatter Rosa, who wanted to be a mother, but with well-dressed daughters. Not being able to show off the unfortunate creature, she blamed her for the hard confinement in which she lived, to take care of her. Little by little she became less assiduous and solicitous with her daughter, she also abandoned caring for her husband, and rejected, without patience to wait for better times or resignation to come to terms with poverty, she only found fleeting relaxation in the reading of novels and in the conversation with her friends and cousins.

The benevolent relatives of old might have helped her in her hardships, but Juan said: "As long as I find what we need to eat, I will receive no alms from anyone". So, when Rosa received some money, it was without Juan knowing about the gift. But how to use those few pesos in dresses and caps, if Juan was aware of the meager funds she had? Some purchases passed as gifts, but even in this form they disgusted Juan. "I don't want", he used to say to his wife, "that you dress with the gifts of other people. I wish I had you as luxurious as a queen, but since I can't, be satisfied with dressing decent and clean, like the wife of a poor employee". Rosa said to herself: "So poor and so proud: like everyone else!...". This same haughtiness and the extreme purposeful detachment with which Juan treated his wife's rich relatives aroused unwillingness among them. They didn't let a day pass without saying to Rosa, with tender compassion: "What a bad thing you did marrying Juan! You were better off at home! Above all, with that figure, with those feet, with that face, you were able to get a better husband. Not because yours is bad; nothing like that, but, daughter, he is a wretched man!".

And little by little these compassionate words, the difference between what was dreamt and what was real, the continuous contemplation of the opulence of others and the Romance readings to which she devoted herself with so much effort produced in Rosa a deep displeasure of life and even a certain resentment or antipathy to the miserable Juan, responsible and author of his misfortune. Rosa tried to spend as many hours outside the house as possible, to live the lavish and borrowed life to which she had been accustomed since she was a child, to talk about dances and scandals and even –why not?– to listen without malice the courtship of some aristocratic wooer. After six months following this way, what had to happen happened: Rosa stepped out of line with her cousin.

Juan did not fall from the seventh heaven like Lucifer. He still kept the embers of the loving bonfire that had inflamed him before, but he did not esteem nor could he ever respect Rosa. He had thought her frivolous, dissipated, presumptuous and vain, but never perverse and criminal. And Rosa –let's do her full justice– did not commit a fault to punish Juan or to enjoy adultery, but out of vanity and confusion. Juan, calm in his anger, left the desecrated home and the city with his daughter. Why should he take revenge? Time and only time, that inexorable vigilante, avenges the crimes of the heart.

He fled from Mexico city, as one flees from the plagued cities. He did not want to suffer the laughter of some and the commiserations of others. Above all, he wanted to educate his daughter, who was two years old at the time, far from the formidable temptations. "Vanity is contagious leprosy", he said to himself, "perhaps hereditary! I want my daughter to grow up in the pure atmosphere of the fields: birds will teach her to be a good mother". In the first days of absence, the girl woke up saying with a weak voice: "Mommy! Mommy!".

How poor Juan suffered when he heard her! He embraced her in his little bed, and, wetting with tears the blond curls and the rosy complexion of the little girl, he said to her sobbing: "Poor thing! We are orphans!".

A year after this, Rosita's mother died; Juan lived working a lot, serving as a teacher in several villages and helping himself with painting and music. Ten months before the beginning of this story he moved to San Antonio, the main town in the valley described in the previous chapter. There he educated some children, painted pious images that he used to sell in the chapels of the haciendas and played the organ on Sundays and the mandatory holidays.

The latter earned him the nickname "Don Juan el Organista". Everyone loved him for his gentleness, good treatment and fame as a learned man. But what made him particularly sympathetic was the immense affection he had for his daughter, That man was father and mother in one piece, with what meticulous solicitude he cared for and attended to the little one! It was worthy to see when he prepared her and clothed her, with the excellence that only women have; when he said the evening prayers to her and he was at the head of the bed until the little girl fell asleep!

Rosita gained a great deal in beauty. When she turned five years old, when this story began, she was the living portrait of her mother. The neighbors argued over the girl and often gave her new clothes and toys. So Rosita always walked like a porcelain doll. And to tell the truth, she was very pretty, very discreet, very cute and very funny, as to eat her with kisses!

Now let's see what Don Juan the Organist went to look for in the neighboring ranch de la Cruz.

III

–Go ahead, my friend Don Juan, come in.

Juan took off his hat respectfully and entered the ranch's office. It was a quite large room with windows opening to the field and a corral. Its furniture consisted of a large, rough table, placed at the bottom, just below the picture of Our Lady of Guadalupe. The table carpet was of green color; a black rag hung from one of its corners, put there to clean the feathers; and on top, placed with much order, the ledgers were piled, very orderly, presided over by the classic copper inkwell still used by the parish notaries. A few chairs with seats of tule[1], completed the furniture, and either lying or leaning on them, whether cornered or raised to the parapets of the windows, there were also stirrups, chaps, saddles, moldy swords, spurs and carbines. A very peculiar smell of horsehair and old leather escaped from all this.

Don Pedro Anzúrez, owner of the ranch, wrote in a large book with a bird's feather, because he had never been able to come to terms with modern ones. From the place where Juan was standing, you could see the wide and round penmanship of Don Pedro, but Juan did not pay attention to the strokes and features of the pen: with the felt hat in his hand he waited to be invited to sit down.

–Rest yourself and don't bother with compliments, said Don Pedro, interrupting his writing.

And he continued as serious and burdensome as before, adding lines and more lines of writing and stopping from time to time to do some sums in a low voice. Then he closed the leather-wrapped ledger, put the feather in a cup full of ammunition, and, turning to Juan, he said so:

–My friend, bring over the chair and let's talk... That's it! Don't you want a cigarette?

–Thank you, Don Pedro, I don't smoke.

–The priest will have informed you briefly of what I intend.

–Indeed, the father told me last night that you intended to employ me in your house as a preceptor for the children.

–That's it. You will have noticed that I have a particular esteem for you, not only because of the knowledge that everyone, without exception, grants you, but also because of the Christian virtues, so rare in today's young people, and which make you sympathetic to my eyes. You are industrious, humble, faithful to the law of God, honest to the letter and a loving father like few others. Come on! I like you! Since we became friends on the

---

1 A generic name for several species of long-stemmed plants, the fibers of which are used to weave chair seats.

occasion of the feast of Carmen, when you played the organ in my chapel, I have understood that you are out of your natural place, and that a man of such painstaking education deserves better luck and the help of all those who think like me. So you have no qualms about admitting what I propose? Do you accept?

–With soul and life, Don Pedro.

–Now we're going to deal with the mercantile matters. You'll have a house, food and fifty pesos a month. Of course, you will come with your daughter. My wife and my two older daughters love the girl very much, and they will treat you as a person of the family. The duties of the preceptor are as follows: to teach my two boys arithmetic, a little grammar, French and bookkeeping. Agreed?

–Don Pedro, you fill me with favors. I can hardly get the sum you offer me in the village, and from that I have to pay the rent of the house, the daily cost of the expenses and the lighting. How then, not to admit with joy what you offer to me?

–Then let's turn over a new leaf. Your place will be the one you already know... next to the administrator's piece. It is not very big; it consists of two rooms quite wide and well ventilated. Besides, you can use the whole house. More than as an employee, as a friend. So when can you move in?

–Tomorrow, if you like.

–No, tomorrow is Sunday and it's not good to work on your relocation. It will be Monday.

Don Pedro got up from his armchair. John, confused, said goodbye, and so ended, with joy for both of them, the interview.

IV

I will not paint Juan's life at the ranch de la Cruz. He worked from nine to twelve with the children, ate with the family, and in the afternoons went for a walk or to read on the garden bench. Little by little, everyone in the house became fond of him; but without such signs of affection emboldening him or upsetting him, as is usually the case for those who, out of pride, believe they deserve everything. Juan considered that he was a poor employee of Don Pedro, and that, as such, he should treat him with respect, the same as the rest of the family. And the truth is that not even with a torch would you find people simpler or nicer than the wife and daughters of Don Pedro. There was not a shred of pride in those souls of incomparable gentleness. Juana, the eldest daughter, was a little cranky. She was also the one who carried the weight of the house and had to deal with the servants. But her impatience and anger were always as fleeting as lightning. Enriqueta had a greater sweetness of character. And as for the lady, charitable, frank, intelligent, she deserved to be as happy as she was.

Juan thanked Don Pedro and his family, rather than the distinction with which they treated him, for the affection they had shown Rosita.

Enriqueta, particularly, was the most tender with the girl. She looked like a mother; but a doubly august mother: mother and virgin. Many times, Juan tried to put a prudent stop to such pampering, fearful, perhaps with good reason, that the girl would become accustomed and arrogant. But what father does not see with joy the happiness of his daughter? What happened was that, gradually, those requests of Enriqueta, that tender care awoke in Juan a soft love, hidden first under the disguise of gratitude, but later so great, so deep and so violent, as hidden, silent and repressed. The continuous treatment, the daily touch of those good and loving souls gave fuel to the intense passion of the unfortunate preceptor. But Juan knew perfectly how impossible his dream was. He was there in a humble condition, welcomed, it is true, with much esteem, but distant from the woman he loved, as far away as are the lakes from the sun. Did he know, perhaps, what were the purposes of his parents? She had been carefully instructed and educated, not for the companion of a poor man who could give her nothing outside of love, but to be the wife of a man placed in a dignified and superior category. If he were to speak of love, he would be like the man whom they entertain out of kindness in a house, and, taking advantage of the favorable occasion, steals some jewel. No, Juan would not. To correspond in such a way to the favors that Don Pedro had done him, would have been a lack of nobility. A thousand times, however, love, which is a great sophist, said to him in a very low voice: "Why not?".

V

Juan understood well the impossibility of keeping his love hidden for a long time; but, fearful and convinced of his own misfortune, he deliberately postponed the day of the inevitable confession. Alone, in the darkness of his bedroom or in the silence of the garden, he imagined it easy and possible what later seemed unfeasible to him. But, as we are always inclined to believe what pleases us, little by little the idea that his dreams were not at all unachievable, as he suspected at first, gained ground in his understanding. This moral transformation seemed to be favored by Enriqueta's continuous requests, more and more tender and kind to Rosita and more and more kind to the poor Juan. He interpreted such signs of affection as signs of love, and even believed –so easy it is to give ear to the presumptuous vanity– that Enriqueta loved him and that sooner or later he would fulfill his dreams. What did Juan count on to ascend to that heaven seen in his hallucinations and ecstasies? With the great accomplice of lovers and dreamers: with the unexpected.

The worst thing for Juan was the intimate treatment he received from Enriqueta. He lived in her atmosphere and felt her love without possessing it, as wine-makers get drunk with the smell of wine they don't drink. Every day Juan found a new charm in his beloved woman. It was as if he were attending the boudoir of her soul and seeing all the veils that covered her fall one by one. Besides, there is nothing so invincibly seductive as a beautiful woman in the abandonment of intimate life. Juan looked at Enriqueta as she came out of the bedroom, her cheeks still warm from the long contact of the pillow. And he also saw her with her hair loose or lying on her mother's knees. And every attitude, every movement, every gesture discovered new beauties in her. And so was the growth of his admiration for the moral beauty of Enriqueta. All those virtues that seek darkness to shine and that the profane never can guess; all those irresistible attractions that the woman hides, avaricious, to the strangers and that only the family enjoys increased the esteem of Juan and his affection. In addition, those two lives had a point of coincidence: Rosita. Enriqueta lavished on the girl all the tenderness and care of a young mother; of a mother who was at the same time like the older sister of her daughter. Once the girl fell ill. It was necessary to call a doctor from Mexico, whose trip was paid for by Don Pedro. Enriqueta did not abandon the sick girl for a single moment.

She watched over her several nights; when she saw Juan faint with pain, she said to him, affectionately:

–Don't despair. We will save her. I have already begged our Mother of Light to let us keep her. Come and pray the novena with me.

The girl was healed, but the wretched Juan had worsened. Precisely on the day the doctor discharged her, Juan went to the dining room of the hacienda. They had already served the soup when Don Pedro said aloud:

–Today is a doubly exhausting day. Rosita is convalescing and Carlos arrives at the hacienda. Then, bowing to Juan's ear, he added:

–My friend, we don't have any secrets for you, because you're already part of the family: Carlos is Enriqueta's boyfriend.

VI

How! Enriqueta had a boyfriend! Behold, the unexpected, that great accomplice in whom Juan trusted, turned against him. And when? When after that illness of the girl, during which Enriqueta had divided with him the anxieties and the cares, his passion was more alive and more intense.

Juan thought he was dying of anguish, and when he returned to his room and saw his daughter stretching out her squalid arms, he exclaimed, as in those supreme moments that followed the abandonment of his wife:

–Oh, poor daughter, you no longer have a mother!

Wasn't Enriqueta Rosita's mother? She was also going to leave her an orphan, like the other, when she went away with a man whom Juan did not know yet, but whom he hated. Who was that Carlos? Probably a rich man... The poor always put those they hate at fault. Handsome! Juan was not and instinctively understood that his rival's triumph was due to the qualities he lacked. Intelligent... "No, not intelligent", whispered Juan.

Little by little, the unfortunate preceptor was seeing reality more distinctly. And it began to be clearly explained how many gestures, actions and words of Enriqueta were mistakenly interpreted favorably by his passion. It was a thaw of illusions. The sun warmed the snow statue with its rays, and the figure fell apart. Juan said to himself:

How a fool I was! I had a treasure of glances, smiles and words; that is, diamonds, pearls and gold. And now a foreigner comes to me, comes up to me and says with an imperious tone: "Give me back what you possess. None of that is yours. It is all mine. Do you remember the blush that dyed her face when, before you, they asked her if she loved anyone? You imagined that blush to be the shadow of your soul and it was but the heat of mine. One evening you found her alone in the garden and she ran so that you wouldn't see her. She's running away from me, because she knows my affection –you said to yourself–. Poor fool! She dodged you to hide the letter that I wrote her, that she was going to read with her lips. And those wet glances of love that she directed to your face some nights, were addressed to me. Even when she caressed your daughter's little head, she was thinking of the children we would have and, therefore, of me as well. All the memories you have are stolen. Give me back your jewels one by one".

And he became poorer and naked. Until at last his legs flinched and he fell fainting to the ground.

Juan did not die of sorrow, because death never took pity of the unhappy. On the night of that terrible day Carlos arrived at the hacienda; Juan did not want to go down to the dining room, but from his room, seated at the head of the bed where his convalescent daughter slept, he could hear the noise of the dishes and the cheerful laughter of the diners. What would Carlos be like? Curiosity drove Juan to go out quietly and spy through the hole in the key. But the repugnance that Enriqueta's boyfriend inspired him and his depressed mood stopped him. Soon the noise ceased; Juan heard the footsteps of the newcomer who was humming a mazurca[2] across the courtyard; the conversation of the servants who were cleaning the dishes in the kitchen and then... woman's footprints that were approaching. Then he remembered. Enriqueta was used to go every night and before going to bed to see her sick girl and take care of her well. She was going into the bedroom! Juan only had time to hide his head in his arms, lying on the bed, and pretend he was sleeping. Why should he see her? Above all, weeping

---

2 A lively Polish dance resembling the polka.

can be suffocated while one is not speaking; but words open up, when one speaks, the prison of tears, and these tears escape.

Enriqueta tiptoed in and, seeing Juan there, she hesitated a few moments before approaching the bed. At last he approached. With much care and trying to make as little noise as possible, she covered the girl well with his bedspreads. Then she bent down to kiss the sick girl on the cheeks and forehead. Juan heard the sound of kisses and felt the tip of Enriqueta's breasts touching one of his arms. Her eyes were tightly closed and he bit his lips. When the noise of Enriqueta's footsteps was gradually lost in the sonorous passageway, Juan began to cry.

VII

Why would we describe one by one his sufferings? Three months after that horrible night, Enriqueta was getting married in the chapel of the ranch. Juan, who had not played the organ in a long time, was going to play it during the religious ceremony. On the eve of that solemn day Don Pedro said to the unfortunate preceptor:

–Tomorrow, my friend, is a feast day for the family. Carlos is a good boy and will make Enriqueta happy. If not for that consideration, I assure you that we would be very sad... You see... Enriqueta is the joy of the house and she's leaving us! But we have to renounce selfishness and see for the future of our own. These separations are necessary in life. I want the wedding to be solemn. You will see, my friend, you will see what a wedding basket her mother has prepared for the girl. I'm already losing my head and I'm stunned by so many preparations. We are marrying Enriqueta in the chapel, to save us the commitments we would have had in Mexico city; but it was necessary, however, to invite the closest relatives and close friends. And you've probably noticed the hubbub of the house. There is no empty corner. But, to all this, I forgot to tell you the most urgent thing. I want you to play the organ for us tomorrow, my friend Don Juan. I know you do wonders. The organ in the chapel is not very good, but I ordered it to be tuned. So can I trust your goodness?

Juan accepted. He had thought not to spend the day in the house; to go with any pretext to the village, to the mountain, to a place where he would be alone. But it was necessary for him to drain the chalice. Welcome! He was going to play the organ in the marriage of his beloved. What a bitter irony!

He spent the previous day locked in his room. What a day that was! As he passed through one of the rooms to go to Don Pedro's desk, which had summoned him, Juan saw Enriqueta's wedding basket on the table. Coincidentally, the mother was near and wanted to show Juan the nice things who guarded that delicate wicker basket. And Juan saw everything: the very fine batiste handkerchiefs, the pearl necklace, the Brussels lace, the transparent and embroidered shirts, which seemed to have been woven by the angels.

At last the day of the wedding dawned; Juan, who had not been able to close his eyes all night, went to the chapel, still dark and silent. He helped to light the candles and fix the benches. After the task was finished, he climbed into the choir; Rosita accompanied him. The poor girl was sad. Enriqueta had forgotten her because of a boyfriend and the preparations for her marriage. Moreover, with the insight of the girls who have suffered, Rosita guessed that her father was suffering.

From the choir you could look at the chapel from one end to the other. Little by little it was filled with guests. Through the window overlooking the courtyard you could see the double row of the ranch's workers, formed into compact battalions. At seven o'clock the bride and groom, accompanied by their godparents, entered the chapel. How beautiful Enriqueta was! She looked like an angel dressed with her own wings. They knelt on the steps of the altar; the priest came out of the sacristy, preceded by the golden cross and the candles; the presbytery was filled with the aromatic cloud of incense and the ceremony began. Juan first played a march of triumph. It would have been said that the notes came from the narrow pipes of the organ, on horseback, sounding the trumpets and waving the flags in cadence. It was a solemn, almost warlike harmony, a triumphal bow made with sounds, under which the arrogant betrothed passed. From time to time, a shy and complaining melody slipped like a black thread on that cloth of golden notes. It looked like the voice of a slave, attached to the victor's chariot. In that fugitive and mournful melody was revealed Juan's affliction, similar to an enormous reservoir of water from which only a faint stream escapes. Afterwards, the harmonious waves curled, like the biblical lake of Tiberias. The main theme jumped on the shaky surface, like the fishermen's boat shaken by the waves. Sometimes a wave covered it and for brief moments it was buried and invisible. But then, overcoming the storm, he appeared again graceful, young and gallant, like a warrior who penetrates, sword in hand, between the enemy squadrons, and comes dripping blood, but alive.

That strange accompaniment was an improvisation. Juan played by translating his pains; he was the only author of that harmony similar to a flight of spirits in sorrow, imprisoned before in the tubes. When they were violently fired from the metal cannons, the notes twisted and complained. At that moment, the priest with gray hair joined his white hands of the bride and groom.

Then the storm calmed down. Christ appeared standing on the waves of the furious lake, whose turbulent waves calmed down. An immense sadness, an infinite melancholy succeeded the storm. And then the melody softened: it was a sea, but a calm sea, a sea of tears. On that smooth surface floated Juan's aching soul. The poor musician thought of his dead illusions, of his crazy dreams, and cried very much like the child who, afraid of being reprimanded, hides his little head in a corner. In the melodic tenderness, the sobs, the monotonous songs of the slaves and the very sad tone of the "praised" were joined. He saw Enriqueta in his mind, just as he saw her the first night he spent in the ranch, there, in that same chapel, today so resplendent and adorned. He saw her praying the rosary, wrapped in a dark blue shawl. He well remembered: when everyone went out step by step, Enriqueta, who was the last one to get up, approached the picture of the Virgin of Light, hanging on one of the walls, and touched with her lips the rosy soles of the image. How much poor Juan had loved her! It is over! What to live for? There she was, luxurious and elegant next to her boyfriend, smiling with happiness. And each time the melody was sadder. At the moment of the elevation, the bells rang and many birds gurgled in the warheads. It was the page who was forced to sing and who, determined, threw the lute, saying: "I don't want any more!". But, little by little, the music, whipped by the angry hand of the master, sounded more melancholic than before. Until at last, when the Mass was over, the conjured and rabid notes exploded again in an immense explosion of anger. And in the midst of that confusion, in the tumult of that escape of mutilated harmonies and wounded notes, a cry was heard. The air continued to vibrate for brief moments. It looked like a grumbling giant. And then the choir was silent, the organ mute, and instead of triumphal melodies or hymns, the sobs of a little girl were heard.

It was Rosita crying without consolation, hugging her father's corpse.

Lady of Hearts

There, under the tall trees of the French Pantheon, sleeps the poor blonde-haired woman, whom I loved for a week... A whole century!... and she married another one.

Many times, when, tired and bored with the hustle and bustle, I choose the picturesque streets of the Pantheon for my evening walks, I find the delicate marble urn in which the one that will never return rests. Yesterday I was surprised by the night in those places. It was beginning to rain and an icy air moved the flowers of the cemetery. Quickly looking for the exit, I found the tomb of the poor deceased woman. I stopped for a moment, and as I looked at the slabs moistened by the rain, I said, with deepest sadness:

–Poor thing! How cold she would be on the marble of her bed!

Rosa-Thé was, in fact, as cold as a Creole from Havana. How many times I hastened to throw the fur hood on her naked white shoulders, at the exit of some dance! How many times I saw her in a corner of the couch, hiding her arms, numb, under the folds of a wool coat! And now, there she is, under the marble tombstone that the rain wets unceasingly! Poor thing!

***

When Rosa-Thé got married, her parents thought she was going to be very happy. I never believed it, but I reserved my opinions, fearful that they would attribute this to spite. The truth is that by the time Rosa-Thé got married, I had stopped loving her, at least with the liveliness of the first days. However, the marriage of an old flame is never very funny. It's like a tooth being pulled out of us.

Above all, what increased my displeasure was the deep conviction that she was going to be unhappy. It made me furious when I heard the smiling prophecies of her family. How! That Pedro would be a good husband? But don't these people know –I said to myself– that Pedro is a gambler? They attribute such a serious vice to the dismal idleness; they believe that once he is married, he will make amends... but gamblers don't amend themselves.

And I would have seen, if not with joy, with resignation at least, the marriage of Rosa-Thé with a good boy. But the opposite of a well is a tower; the opposite of a bridge, an aqueduct; the opposite of a good husband, that was Pedro. Not because he lacked personal clothing, health, money, or affection for poor Rosa-Thé, but because that roguish vice had to follow him eternally, like a creditor who was never paid.

Rosa-Thé didn't know Pedro was gambling. In the first months of marriage, he was, with effect, the most submissive and obsequious thing that could be desired for the quiet life of the home. But, alas, in a short time, the piquant custom dragged him to the green carpet. Then began the pretexts for spending the nights outside the house, the bitterness of character, the shortness and the sudden disappearance of money. Once upon a time, Rosa was preparing to attend a dance. Pedro was already properly dressed, waiting in the cabinet for his wife. But since she was absorbed still in her toilette, which took her a very long time, Pedro opened partially the door of the dresser and said to Rosa:

–Look, while you finish your hair, I'm going to smoke in the open air. I'll be back in half an hour. It was half past nine. At ten o'clock Rosa was ready to dance. She sat on a small armchair and waited. The fourth, the middle, the three quarters sounded, and Pedro didn't come back. Then she began to get concerned. What would have happened to him? At every moment she looked out onto the balcony, squeezing his gloves and handkerchief. Would a carriage have hit him? He's so careless! –Rosa said. Could he have had a fight with anyone? No one is free of enemies! Above all, there are so many evildoers in the street! And anticipating the events with her impatient imagination, she imagined seeing her husband coming on an stretcher with a broken leg or even dead. And her anguish became more and more acute, so much so that at eleven o'clock she sent one boy to look for him in the streets, and then another, then three, until the boy and the lackey, the coachman, the doorman, and all the men in the servitude, searched for him in the streets and coffee houses without leaving a meeting point without searching, without stopping their searches for a moment.

The servants arrived fatigued and without any news of their master; later they left with new orders and always returned the same as they left. Finally, after midnight, Rosa ordered to get ready the carriage. She was going to look for Pedro. At full escape, the horses left the hallway. Rosa knocked at the door of many houses; the hurried lackey stepped down, and after conferring with the doormen, he would then go up to the coachman's seat, and the carriage would be driven again through the streets as quickly as possible. At about one o'clock, Rosa passed through a street and saw open and illuminated the balconies of a house. It had to be a club or something like that. Would Pedro be in that place? The car stopped, and the lackey, without needing to knock, because the door was ajar, entered the courtyard; he climbed the stairs and, a little while later, he came back down them even faster. He arrived at the door of the carriage, through which the livid countenance of Rosa could be seen, and said, with the satisfaction of the one who brings the long-awaited news:

–The master is upstairs: he is gambling... He says he can't come... that he'll came back to the house later.

And, indeed, at six o'clock in the morning, Pedro appeared in the lady's rooms. The unhappy woman had spent the night without sleep, sitting there in that armchair, watching, with the fixed gaze of a madwoman, on the hands of the clock that revolved around the dial, still dressed in her dance costume, with flowers in her hair and on her chest. Every time footsteps were heard in the street, Rosa-Thé looked out onto the balcony. But they were the footsteps of the gendarme or some drunk who staggered back home. And the stars were shining less and the roosters singing more. From time to time, Rosa heard the sound of a carriage: it was the sound of one of her friends coming back from the dance. Little by little, the light, first shy and white, spread all over the sky. A stagecoach passed by the corner and the bells of La Profesa calling for Mass were heard. Rosa did not want to stay on the balcony any longer. What would those who saw her say? In addition, her teeth clashed with each other, and an unpleasant shiver crept into her body. Rosa, so weak, so cowardly and so cold, had spent a good part of the morning on the balcony, and what's worse, in a dance costume, with her shoulders and throat uncovered.

She was so possessed with pain that she did not notice the lightness of her costume. Only when the light, abruptly entering through the paired doors of the balcony, went to portray her in the mirror of the wardrobe, did Rosa see herself dressed for the party and covered with flowers, like a virgin whom they take to the grave. Then, huddled in the armchair, covering her shoulders with a cap, she started to cry. She had thought about having so much fun in that dance! Because Rosa was, after all, a little girl. She had become so pretty, not to captivate others, but for Pedro to wear her with pride! And instead of the party, the anguish, the anguish, and then... then the horrible certainty that her husband, with no mercy for her pains, left her at the gates of a gambling house, where she was probably ruined. Rosa was crying like a child, and little by little she was pulling out of her hair the flowers that so beautifully adorned her. And so an hour went by, listening to the sound of brooms and the conversations of the street sweepers.

At last, she heard Pedro's footsteps. Yes, it was him! She wiped her tears hastily, she was ashamed of having cried, anger overcame the pain in her mood and she was ready to fight, to let off steam, to justly rebuke her husband. But... in vain! Pedro's look disarmed her; he came livid, collapsed, with the eyes of a man who has lost his reason, the bow of his white tie was undone and his hair bristling. He could hardly speak.

–You're right... I'm a miserable... I've lost everything... your carriages, your jewels... my horses... We have nothing! I have ruined you! I have ruined you! I am a scoundrel!

Rosa-Thé's anger dissipated like the shadows at dawn. Faced with that immense misfortune, she wanted to recover her cold blood. She was so good! An immense tenderness replaced the hard phrases with which she proposed to receive her husband. And embracing his neck, bringing Pedro's disheveled head closer to her breast, she attracted him and they cried together for a long time, while the light, indifferent to everything, jumped with joy and was seen in the mirrors, furniture and stained glass windows.

Rosa accepted poverty with great courage. They had to look for a humbler house, renounce to the carriage, fire almost all the servants, replace the satin of the furniture with cretonne and cheap fabrics; to live, in short, like the family of a poor employee who earns eighty pesos every month. But Rosa put such art into everything, she economized so much with her vigilance and her work, she was so decisive and so cheerful, that Pedro felt less the terrible burden of poverty. At first, Pedro, ashamed of himself and proud of his wife, dedicated himself with soul and life to his work. And Rosa was happier than before, because he no longer left at night and because she always saw him by her side.

However, this happiness did not last very long. Pedro reunited with certain friends who dragged him back into the game. He could no longer bet large amounts as before, but he could bet two, five, or ten pesos. First he excused himself, saying in his conscience, "I do no evil. Now that I have nothing, that's when I have to gamble. I have to find a way to get my wife out of the precarious situation we live in. The game owes me my entire fortune. I'm going to get it back".

And he began again to invent peremptory occupations, and to spend a good part of the nights out of his house. It didn't take long for Rosa to discover the truth. The meager sums Pedro earned –which were enough to cover their small budget– were not enough lately. Convinced that this vice was incurable and radical in her husband, she fell into the deepest despondency. What to fight for? Without listening to her advice or listening to her supplications, nor appreciating her cares and works, Pedro abandoned her for playing cards.

A terrible consumption took hold of her. She no longer laughed, she no longer sang, she lost the fresh colors of her complexion, the brightness of her eyes, the grace of her uncluttered movements, and she lost weight little by little. After a few months she fell into bed.

The doctors said that they could not cure her illness; and indeed, the only one able to alleviate it was her husband. The husband, instinctively understanding that he was the cause of the illness, made amends in those days, and looking for prize money, borrowing from his friends, he obtained the necessary resources to take care of the sick woman. He brought her the best doctors and bought all the medicines no matter how expensive they were. One doctor hit the nail on the head, apparently (saving my readers the meticulous description of the illness), and said: –This is cured only by such and such medicines.

Pedro bought them and, with good effect, Rosa-Thé visibly improved. Why did she got worse afterwards? This is what neither Pedro nor the doctor could explain. The medicines were infallible and had had a wonderful effect at first. What, then, was the cause of the relapse? Only I know, and I'm going to tell. Rosita told me the night she died, while I was watching over her, because we had become good friends again.

–I don't want to be cured –she said–. You know everything, the sadness and anguish that I have gone through, the invincible force of that vice that I detest and that dominates Pedro, my love for him and my detachment from life. I am so happy being sick! Pedro doesn't gamble, he spends his days at the head of my bed, and when I'm sick and close my eyes, pretending to sleep, I hear that he sobs and I feel the humidity of his tears in my hand. Now he loves me, now he doesn't abandon me, now he takes care of me with the tender requests of a mother. If I am relieved, he will escape again, he will seek, far from me, the emotions of the game. I will no longer have him by my side nor will I feel his lips on my forehead. He will go away, as he has gone so many times, leaving me very sad and lonely. If I die, perhaps the memory of his poor victim will separate him from the path he is on. No, I don't want to be relieved. I want to be sick for a long time. That's why, when he brings me medicine, I resort to some pretext to stay alone, and then I spill the elixir on the floor...

***

There, under the tall trees of the French Pantheon, sleeps the poor thing of blonde hair whom I loved for a week... A whole century!... and she married another.

Rip-Rip

I didn't see this story, but I think I dreamt it.

What things the eyes see when they are closed! It seems it is impossible for us to have so many people and so many things inside... because, when the eyelids fall, the gaze, like a lady who closes her balcony, enters to see what is in her house. Well, this house of mine, this house of the lady who looks at me, or has me, is a palace, it is a country house, it is a city, it is a world, it is the universe..., but a universe in which the present, the past and the future are always present. Judging by what I look at when I sleep, I think to myself, and even to you, my readers: "Jesus! What a thing for the blind to see!". Those who are always asleep, what will they see? Love is blind, they say. And love is the only one who sees God.

Who is the author of Rip-Rip's legend? I understand that Washington Irving picked it up, to give it a literary form in one of his books. I know that there is a comic opera with its own title and the same plot. But I haven't read the story of the American novelist and historian nor have I heard the opera... but I have seen Rip-Rip.

If suppositions were not sinful, I would say that Rip-Rip must have been the son of the monk Alefo. This monk was German, easy-going, phlegmatic and I even presume something deaf; a hundred years passed by, without him noticing it, hearing the song of a bird. Rip-Rip was more Yankee, less fond of music and more whiskey drinker: he slept for many years.

Rip-Rip, the one I saw, fell asleep, I don't know why, in some cave he entered... who knows what for.

But he didn't sleep as much as the Rip-Rip of the legend. I think he slept ten years... maybe five... maybe one... anyway, his dream was quite short: he slept badly. But the fact is that he got too old, because that is what happens to those who dream a lot. And since Rip-Rip didn't have a watch, and even if he did, he wouldn't have wound it every twenty-four hours; since calendars hadn't been invented, and since there are no mirrors in the woods, Rip-Rip couldn't notice the hours, days, or months that had passed while he was sleeping, nor could he know that he was already an old man. It almost always happens: a long time before one knows one is old, others know it and say it.

Rip-Rip, still a little sleepy and ashamed to have spent an entire night out of his house –he who was a believing and practicing husband– said to himself, not without shock: "Let's go home!".

And there goes Rip-Rip with his very gray beard (which he thought was very blonde) barely crossing those almost inaccessible paths! And no, it was the effect of old age, which is not the sum of years, but the sum of dreams!

Walking, walking, Rip-Rip thought: "Poor little woman of mine! How alarmed she will be! I can't explain what happened. I must be sick... very sick. I went out at dawn... it's dawn now... so I spent day and night outside the house. But what did I do? I don't go to the tavern; I don't drink... No doubt I was surprised by the illness in the mountain and I fell senselessly in that grotto... She must have looked everywhere for me... How could she not, if she loves me so much and is so good? She must not have slept... She'll be crying... And to come alone, at night, for these twists and turns! Although alone... no, she didn't have to come alone. In the village they love me well, I have many friends... mainly Juan from the mill. Surely, seeing her affliction, everyone will have helped her to look for me... Juan mainly. But what about the little girl, my daughter? Will they bring her? At such hours? In this cold? It may well be, because she loves me so much, and she loves her daughter so much, and she loves both of us so much, that she wouldn't leave her alone for anyone, nor would she stop looking for me for anyone. How reckless! Will it hurt her? Anyway, the first thing is that she... but which one is she?...".

And Rip-Rip walked and walked... and he couldn't run.

He finally reached the village, which was almost the same... but not completely. The parish tower seemed whiter to him, the mayor's house looked taller, the main shop looked as if it had another door, and the people he saw as seemed to have different faces. Would he still be half asleep? Would he still be sick?

The first friend he found was the priest. It was him: with his green umbrella; with his high hat, which was the highest of all the neighborhood; with his breviary, always closed; with his coat, which was always a cassock.

–Mister priest, good morning.

–Excuse me, son.

–It wasn't my fault, Father... I didn't get drunk... I didn't do anything wrong... My poor wife's...

–I told you to excuse me. And go: go somewhere else, because there are plenty of beggars here.

Why did the priest talk to him like that? He'd never asked for alms. He didn't give for worship, because he didn't have any money. He didn't attend the Lenten sermons, because he worked all day, overnight. But he went to the seven o'clock mass every feast day, and confessed and received communion every year. There was no reason for the priest to treat him with contempt. There was no reason!

And he let him go without saying anything, because he was tempted to hit him... and he was the priest.

With a step lightened by anger Rip-Rip followed his path. Fortunately the house was very close... He could already see the light from his windows... And since the door was farther away than the windows, he approached the first one of these to knock, to tell Luz: Here I am! Don't rush any more!

There was no need for him to call. The window was open: Luz sewed quietly, and the moment Rip-Rip arrived, Juan –Juan from the mill– kissed her on the lips.

–Are you coming back soon, sonny?

Rip-Rip felt that everything was red around him. Miserable! Miserable!... Trembling like a drunkard or an old man, he entered the house. He wanted to kill: but he was so weak, that when he reached the room where they were talking, he fell to the ground. He couldn't get up; he couldn't speak; but he could keep his eyes open, wide open, to see how the adulterous wife and the traitor friend paled in terror.

And they both paled. A cry from her –the same cry that poor Rip had heard when a thief entered the house– and then Juan's arms that bound him, but not to drown him, but pious, charitable, to lift him off the ground.

Rip-Rip would have given his life, his soul too, to be able to say a word, a blasphemy.

–He is not drunk, Luz; he is sick.

And Luz, though still afraid, approached the unknown vagabond.

–Poor old man! What happens to him? Perhaps he was coming for alms and fell down, exhausted with hunger.

–But if we give him something, it could hurt him. I'll take him to my bed first.

–No, not to your bed, for the wretch is very dirty. I'll call the worker, and between you and him they'll take him to the apothecary.

The girl came in at that moment:

–Mommy, mommy!

–Don't be afraid, my life, it's only a man.

–How ugly, mama! How frightening! It's like a ghost!

And Rip heard.

He could see too, but he wasn't sure what he could see. That little room was the same... his. In that leather and bamboo armchair he sat at night when he came back, tired, after having sold the wheat of his little land in the mill where Juan was the administrator. Those window curtains were his luxury. He bought them at the cost of many savings and sacrifices. That was Juan; that one, Luz... but they were not the same... And the little one was not the little one!

Had he died? Was he crazy? But he felt that he was alive! He listened... he saw... how one hears and sees in nightmares.

They carried him to the apothecary on their shoulders, and left him there, because the girl was afraid of him. Luz went with Juan... and no one was surprised that she took his arm and that she abandoned her husband, almost dying. He couldn't move, he couldn't scream, to say: I'm Rip!

At last, he said it, after many hours, perhaps many years, perhaps many centuries. But they didn't know him: they didn't want to know him.

–You wretch! You're crazy! –said the apothecary.

–We must take him to the mayor because he may be a furious madman –said another.

–Yes, it's true; we'll tie him up if he resists.

And they were going to bound him up, but the pain and the anger had given Rip back his strength. Like a rabid dog, he attacked his executioners, managed to get rid of his arms, and started to run. He went home... He was going to kill! But people followed him, cornered him. It was a hunt and he was the beast.

The instinct of self-preservation overcame everything. The first thing was to leave the village, win the mountain, hide and come back later, at night, to take revenge, to do justice.

There goes Rip like a hungry wolf! There he goes through the most intricate part of the jungle! He was thirsty... the thirst that fires must feel. And he went straight to the spring... to drink, to sink into the water and beat it with his arms... perhaps, perhaps to drown. He approached the stream, and there, on the surface, death came out to receive him. Yes, because it was death, in the form of a man, the image of a decrepit man that appeared in the crystal of the wave! No doubt that livid spectrum was coming for him. He was not of flesh and blood, certainly; he was not a man, because he moved at the same time as Rip, and those movements did not shake the water. He wasn't a corpse, because his hands and arms twisted and twisted. And he wasn't Rip, he wasn't him! He was like one of his grandparents, who appeared to him to take him to his dead father. "But what about my shadow", Rip thought. "Why isn't my body portrayed in that mirror? Why do I see and scream, and the echo of that mountain doesn't repeat my voice, but another unknown voice?".

And there Rip went to look for himself in the bosom of the waves! And the old man, surely, took him with his dead father, because Rip has not returned!

Isn't this an extravagant dream?

I saw Rip very poor, I saw him rich; I saw him young, I saw him old; at times in a woodcutter's hut, sometimes in a house whose windows had white curtains; already seated in that leather and bamboo chair, or on an ebony and satin sofa... he was not a man, there were many men... perhaps all men. I can't explain how Rip couldn't talk; how his wife and friend didn't know him, even though he was so old; why he first escaped from those who wanted to tie him up like a madman, or how many years he was asleep or lethargic in that grotto.

How long did he sleep? How long does it take for the beings we love and who love us to forget us? Is forgetting a crime? Are those who forget evil? You see how good Luz and Juan were when they helped poor Rip, who was dying. The girl was frightened; but we cannot blame her; she did not remember her father. All of them were innocent, all of them were good... and nevertheless, all of this is very sad.

Jesus the Nazarene did well to raise only one man, and he was a man who had no wife, who had no daughters and who had just died. It's good to throw a lot of dirt on corpses.

Sad tale

Why are you asking me for verses? For some time now, my poor imagination, like a flower cut before its time, remained in the black curls of a thick hair, as dark as night and as my soul. Why do you ask me for verses? You know very well that from the lute without ropes no harmonies arise and that from the abandoned nest no chirping arises anymore. Winter came and stripped the trees; the waters of the river where you bathed your brief foot froze, and that house, hidden among the branches of the ash trees, has heard phrases of love that did not pronounce our lips and laughter that did not gladden our souls. It seems that an immense sea separates us.

I have run after love and after glory, as children go after the flirtatious butterfly that mocks their persecution and their cries.

All the roses I found had thorns, and all hearts forgot.

The book of my life has only one page of happiness, and that is yours.

Don't ask me for verses anymore. My soul is like those old birds that can't sing and lose their feathers, one by one, when the end of December blows.

There was a time when I thought that love was absolute and unique. There is only one love in my soul, just as there is only one sun in the sky, he said then. Then I learned, studying astronomy, that there are many suns.

I knocked on the door of many hearts and they didn't open it, because there was no one inside. I'll be back from all the blue countries where gold oranges bloom. I am sick, sad. I only believe in God, in my parents and in you. Don't ask me for verses.

It is necessary, however, that I speak to you and that I tell you one by one about my sorrows. That's why I'm going to write to you, so that you can read my poor letters by the window, and think of the absentee who will never come back. The swallows return, after a long absence, and take refuge in the branches of the pine tree. The compass always points to the North. My heart is looking for you.

What do you want me to talk to you about? Leave out the darkness and make your soul illuminate the brightness of love. We are two islands separated by the sea; but the winds carry my words to you and I guess yours. When the evening falls and the stars begin to shine in space, open the closed folds I send you and listen to the ardent phrases of passion that brings the air to your ears. Imagine that we are alone in the forest, that I forgot all the damage you have done to me, and that at the bottom of the padded sedan, I speak to you of my ambitions and my dreams, hear me, as you listen to the song of the birds, the murmur of the waters, the whisper of the breeze. Let us both speak of frivolous things, that is, of serious things. The afternoon is going to die: the wind barely moves its wings, like a tired bird; the horses that pull the carriage, run towards the house, in search of rest; the shadow is falling slowly... let us take advantage of this moment.

***

A few days ago I was walking in the park, thinking of you. The afternoon was cloudy and my heart was sad.

How things have changed! The carriages that go to the promenade today are not the same as you and I saw. I see new faces behind the glass and I can't find the ones I used to distinguish. Do you remember that blonde we always found in a "trois quarts" at the entrance to the Wood? Well, I'm going to refer you to her novel. She loved much; illusions sang in her soul like a flock of nightingales; she married and was deceived. I still remember how impatient she was the days before her marriage. The night she received the bridal gown, she thought she was crazy with joy. I looked at her in the church the next day, crowned with white orange blossoms, trembling with emotion and tears in her eyes. Who would have told us that this marriage was a burial? They loved each other very much, or at least said so. They were going to realize their illusions; wealth prepared a splendid palace for them, and those of us who stood on the beach watched her depart in a boat of gold, we said: –May God lead her to happiness!

A few months later, I found her husband in a coffee house.

–And Blanca?

–She's sick! It was true, Blanca was sick; Blanca was dying. Enrique let her go in search of easy pleasures, and Blanca, alone in her small bedroom, spent the nights without sleeping, watching how the hands are chased and gathered on the dial of the clock. One night Enrique did not return. The next day, Blanca was paler: she looked like wax.

It would have been believed that the light of dawn, which Blanca saw appearing many times from her balcony, had dyed her face with its lily colors.

–Why doesn't he come? –she asked, probing with her eyes the deep darkness of the street.

And the owls cawed, and the icy air of the dawn wounded his face, and Enrique did not return. Suddenly footsteps sounded in the tiles. Blanca leaned over the railing to see if he would come –frustrated hope! It was a drunk returning home, stumbling over lanterns and doors.

Days, weeks, months went by. Blanca was getting worse every day. The doctors could not cure her illness. Are there doctors of souls?

One night, Blanca told Enrique:

–Don't go. I think I'm going to die. Don't leave me.

Enrique laughed at his fears, and went to the circle where his friends were waiting for him. Who dies in his twenties?

Blanca saw him leave with sadness. Then she stood in front of a mirror, straightened her hair and began to pin orange blossom buttons between her tiny curls.

Two large purple circles surrounded his eyes. They were the violets of death. She immediately called her waitress, put on the white dress she had used for her wedding day, and went to bed. At dawn, when Enrique returned home, he saw the balconies of his bedroom open. Four candles burned around the bed. Blanca was dead.

–Do you see? The worldly life, so bright on the outside, is like the white-washed tombs spoken of in the Gospel. Wealth hides many miseries with its harlequin mantle.

Close your ears to the words of the eternal tempter. Do not aspire to gold, which is as cold as the heart of a coquette. Be good, pray much and love little!

The street musician

Cl-Gît le bruit du vent. Here lies the whisper of the wind. Don't you think this epitaph, conceived by Antipater for Orpheus' tomb, is eloquent? What passes, raising only a very slight noise and is extinguished, as if a stronger one blows it out; what they feel when the erectile leaves tremble, what curls the waves, when they tremble, caught in a sudden shiver; the ephemeral brightness of the blue firefly; the quick kiss of Psyche, that is what is similar to certain fleeting spirits that only produce a vibration, a sparkle, a shudder, a chill and die as if they evaporate.

Do you know something more than a few elegant and melancholic waltzes of Juventino Rosas, beautiful as the lady, already wounded to death, in whose hands, almost diaphanous, put poetry a bouquet of immortal camellias? A schottische[1]... a polka... a dance... another waltz... Rumor of the wind! Some have sad names like foreboding: "ABOVE THE WAVES"... there floats, discolored and crowned with buttercups, the corpse of Ophelia. "To DIE DREAMING"... Longing for those who have lived suffering! And observe that it envelops almost all that dance music a certain faint mist of sadness. It seems to be written for rounds of willis[2]. To the beat of the mazurka the

---

1 The schottische is a partnered country dance that apparently originated in Bohemia.

2 White female spirits wandering through the forest at midnight like ghosts, tormenting the men who get lost in the wilderness.

girls dance in a clearing of the forest; they are happy, and laugh and sing; but the musician is sad.

> *The dance is already being arranged.*
> *And the piper, where is he?*
> *–He's burying his mother.*
> *But he'll be here soon.*
> *–And will he come? –Then what shall he do?*
> *Doing his duty*
> *See him with his bagpipe;*
> *But how will the heart bring*
> *The piper,*
> *The piper of Gijón!*
> *The most talkative girl*
> *–Hurry, he says, hurry!*
> *–And the piper blows and cries*
> *Laughing his face off.*

***

Some nights, at the big dances, tired of the party, fleeing from private conversations and impertinent friends, I've started to think about those poor musicians who:

> *How they win with their hands*
> *Bread for his brothers,*
> *In the grace of the baker*
> *They play with resignation*
> *Like the piper played,*
> *The piper of Gijón.*

Federico Gamboa in his *Impressions and memories*, paints us with very vivid colors that Teófilo Pomar who composed dances and played them, first in some salons; then, in the dances of thunder. Pomar also had its ephemeral moment of happiness, "a honeymoon" –says Gamboa– "enchanting because of its speed and intensity. The room of a hotel turned into a corner of the heaven; in the window, birds and flowers; on the work table, the striped paper, the pen ready; the open piano, waiting for the caresses of its owner; on the bedside table, the food snaked from the nearest inn, with only one glass, to increase the pretexts of kissing; and on the walls, on the furniture, everywhere, she, the beloved woman who laughs at our follies and shares them and lulls and drives us crazy...". Then "in the window, the dead bird, the withered flowers; in the work table, the broken feather, the ballot papers of Montepio; the absent piano, leaving an immense hole; in a chair, she, the beloved woman, who cries our pains and shares them and torments us". To live, Pomar continued playing dances. He entered the dance of thunder with a frown, "as if he had been suddenly awakened from some sweet dream, and he arrived at the piano with such visible signs of bad humor that anyone would have feared an ungrateful harmony, a discordant arpeggio, and instead warm, delicate, voluptuous dances sprang up, the dances that were making him famous, his dances, thought and composed by him, those that fed him and rewarded him, on his own, of so much prose, of so much bitterness. And then he became completely abstracted, he did not respond to anyone; there was a night when he improvised a dance, so, in the middle of the intemperate cries, with the excitement of the unveiled one and of the internal disenchantment, when the dawn smiled from the roof and the oil lamps were extinguished yellowish and gloomy...".

"As soon as he was finished, the attendees surrounded him, disputing him, making him dizzy with kindness, with invitations; everyone wanted to give him a cigarette, a drink, good night. The women hung on his arms, dragged him to the cabinets where chamomile or a cold dinner awaited the consumers, and he thanked, refused the more, pleased the less.

–Thank you, thank you very much; what I want is to rest for a moment...

And he was left alone, leaning on the railings of the desert corridor; one step away from the fictitious and noisy joy of orgies, accustomed to them, to the quarrels they bring, to the illusions they carry with them. There he smoked cigarette after cigarette until people became impatient, they wanted to dance...

–Pomar! Let Pomar come!...".

***

Another musician whom I knew closely, the one with the brown long overcoat and the tall hat like a wet slate, was jealous... and he was right. How long were those nights of dancing for him, which are so brief for fortunate lovers! He was thinking of his poor house, so distant from that palace; of his house, with a low window and a procuring landlady; of the beautiful woman, still young, tired of misery and without children; of the strong and young gallant who saw her, with dazzled eyes, one morning in the parish; and imagining infamies and embarrassments, feeling as if countless pins' legs were running all over her body, she seemed to hear a fresh, dripping laugh, as if from juicy watermelon flesh, and another sardonic, mocking, that burned her ear like a whip. He then played with frenzy, with fury, and the bow of the violin, twisting and twisting on the strings, feigned a rapier tearing, an epileptic and continuous insertion and removal of the entrails of the invisible victim. It is not, madam, a sullen moralist who sees you sideways when you pass dancing near him and hear the phrases of passion that the gallant directs to you; it is not a blessed one who on seeing you would like to cover with his gaze the nakedness of your shoulders: he is a poor musician already old, married to a woman still young!...

***

But, among the street violinists I have known, none of them had more suggestive ideas or an unhappier existence than the one with faded blue eyes; the one who, always wearing other people's clothes, thin and long, cast the shadow of a closed umbrella on the carpets, set to drip by the door.

This was an artist, like Juventino Rosas. He was the specter of a rich artist, who existed before him, but was of his family. There are offspring that are apparitions, resurrected ancestors. His lips were always dry, and were thirsty for glory, thirsty for kisses, thirsty for wine.

I still seem to see him, like when I first met him. He plays malagueñas[3] in a student's room. And paints with notes. Don't you see?

How beautiful the singer is! How provocatives are the movements of her hips! How black is her hair! How brief her foot! And how she turns her morbid ankle! With what grace and what malice she sings! These eyes only come out at night, because they are forbidden! When they look, they undress the razor. The arms akimbo seem to say to the handsome man that wants them: –Come and get them!

And that old gypsy who is there with elbows on the table! With his eyes dazzled, his mouth half-open and his legs outstretched, this guy is warming up by the stove, hearing a romping music. He's enjoying a minute as a boy. The chamomile can be seen shining on the glass reeds; the rhythmic clapping can be heard, and the atmosphere is filled with smoke that carries alcohol and, in the alcohol, joy. A razor fell down there; a tambourine rose up there; and in that corner thundered the sonorous kiss that the one with the white blanket, the one with the red rose in her hair, gave to her handsome bullfighter. In the street, Figaro drops his copper bowl to the ground and strums his guitar, while Rosina gets up on tiptoe and opens ajar the balcony door.

Then he plays something very peaceful and melancholic: it's the nightingale that sang on the pomegranate while Julieta stroked Romeo in the dressing room. Love –they tell us– there is still a lot of shadow for the stars to shine brightly and the eyes to say goodbye to more love. An exquisite sweetness is exhaled from their notes; feel the soft contact of the silk scale; see the moon, as if bathing naked in the murmuring and blue waves of the small lake; hear the rumor of the still timid kisses, as if they had just met and known each other; the whisper of curious leaves forming whispers; the fluttering of some birds that cannot sleep because they are in love and

---

3 Flamenco music, something similar to the fandango, with couplets of four octosyllabic verses, characteristic of the province of Málaga in Spain.

want it to be sunrise. The chill of dawn, causes voluptuous goosebumps in our body and the humid and perfumed hair of Juliet rubs our lit cheeks. Dawn already arrived. Don't you see how the lover already comes down from the Gothic window and how the moonbeam shines in the garnet velvet of his jacket and in the golden jewel of his hat? He flees and disappears through the forest of chestnut trees; the stained glass windows are closed and those transparent and fragile notes, those notes that shine like tears and that sound like a crystal shear wounded by the wand of some fairy, are lost and extinguished little by little in the darkness, at dawn. The nightingale no longer sings, but the crystal still weeps.

***

He improvised all that, and upon hearing it, I looked back on the path of life; I would have wanted to be a child again; to sit again on my mother's knees, to kiss the gray hairs of the old man who never, ever dies in the spirit; to hear the bell that called Mass on the day of my first communion; to see the white towers of the church; to believe, to find someone to comfort me as they comforted me when I was not yet suffering... and there goes the brunette Liseta! There goes the little sister who hasn't come back! In that ring the girls dance with the young men; at that table and in the light of a poor lamp, the poet dreams of verses; there goes the grandfather! there goes the bride with whom we thought we had learned to kiss... and we didn't know! there goes everything that went away as the notes go...!

***

The artist who so wonderfully evoked those memories and revived those feelings, used to tell us at the end of playing some of his improvisations:

–This is what I put my soul into, I don't even write it... they don't buy it. You heard the malagueñas; those do produce me, wherever I touch them, applause and a handful of coins. The publisher wants music to be danced, music to be spoiled and stepped on. And I need money for myself and for my vices. These vices disgust me, not because what they are, but because they are degraded, because they are scoundrels. I would like to dignify them, to ennoble them, to clothe them with gold, in the cup, in the woman's body, in the affair. Not take them away from me, for what would I have left? When I am disgusted, I think about killing myself. But there is a certain indefinite fear in me of the other life that remains in my soul, like a grain of unburnt incense in the pot of the censer. Who put it there?... As a child I was an altar boy. Some years ago, that long spectrum, hoffmanesque, that seemed like the shadow of a closed umbrella, died in a hospital, like Juventino Rosas. Many times I have stepped on his music in the dances. Now that I remember it, I feel sorry, as if I had mistreated a child without realizing what I was doing... as if I had trampled fresh petals of soul!

A July 14

(Historical)

I am going to tell you a brief and sad story, and I am going to tell it because today there will be many smiling faces in the streets, and it is good that the happy ones, the cheerful ones, remember that there are some, many unfortunates. It is an episode of July 14, but not of July 14, 1789, but of July 14, 1890. And the heroine is a countrwoman of ours, a beautiful, hapless Mexican. Ah! The newspapers in Paris spoke a lot about her two years ago, more than about Madame Iturbe and her costumes, more than about Miss Escandón and her wedding. Arsenio Houssaye, that old man crowned with roses, dedicated to her a brilliant page, a golden halo, like those that surround the temples of the martyrs. Piety loved her for a moment, just a moment, because piety always has so much to do. And now that I look at those flags, those pennants, those streamers, symbols of noble rejoicing, I think of the poor Mexican woman who passed in Paris on July 14, 1890.

She was married to a Frenchman who came to our land when the evil intervention[1]. Here she had six children... You know that poverty is very fruitful! They lived in hardship, and the husband, hoping to find broader protection in his country, returned to France with his wife and half a dozen creatures. He was a painter, decorated, made squares of flowers and fruits for dining rooms, illuminated portraits, and was willing to admit any hon-

---

1 The Second French Intervention in Mexico, 1861-67. It was an invasion of Mexico, launched by the Second French Empire.

est work. But here's what he couldn't find. Paris is so great! There's so much noise in its streets! It's so hard to hear a man's voice there!

Haughty, proud as he was, he would never have resigned himself to begging. Misery, ever in love with pride, came to accompany him.

One night, exhausted all his resources, he said:

–It is necessary to die.

The youngest of his sons heard him, and then he asked the mother:

–Mother, what is it to die?

–To die, little son, is to go to heaven.

–And what will heaven be like? Will it be like the sea?

–No, heaven is a garden where there are many flowers and many fruits and many toys for children.

–Yes, but they won't be for me. Here, too, there is all that and nothing is mine.

–In heaven they let the children who are not naughty to take whatever they want.

–Mom, let's go to heaven!

The little girl, who listened attentively, then said:

–But the journey must be long, very long? From here to heaven...!

–No, much more comfortable and faster than the one from Mexico to France. You go to sleep, and when you wake up, you're in heaven...!

–And there are celebrations like the one of tomorrow, with fireworks and music?

–All year round.

–Then we'll go.

And those creatures, for whom the earth was so hard, got excited with the idea of going to heaven.

To die! What a beautiful word! It sounded in their ears as it does, singing, in the ears of some men.

–But we're not leaving yet –said another of the children–. Tomorrow is July 14. I want to see the fireworks.

Father and mother crossed a pleading gaze.

– We'll wait!

They had almost forgotten their hunger, hoping to go to heaven, and they fell asleep dreaming of starry darts and white porcelain toys, attended by angels. Only the youngest, who had not understood, said in a faint voice:

–Mom, Dad.

The two spouses looked at each other without speaking. How can we wait until tomorrow?

–I still can, by selling the last thing, collect a franc. Pedro, Juanito wants to see the fires!

And they waited... It would be blasphemy to write: they waited. The father had a little tablet of painted flowers that he had not been able to sell.

He was going to give it to the good lady in the pond. Maybe she would give him something!

Very early, he went. The feast was already singing its triumphal anthem in squares and boulevards.

Soon the door of the tiny room was opened again, and the painter came back.

–What did they give you?

He, defeated, without unfolding his lips, dropped a few stamps on the floor.

–For the children to have fun. Don't you remember the story of Schiavone? That Venetian painter also had a wife, six children and hunger. He was also superb. And he painted I don't know what for the Fathers of Santa Croce; he went to give up his work and the Fathers gave him a bouquet of roses as a reward. He also dropped the flowers on the naked dais, and the white Giacinta, his wife, stripped them into the empty plates, and when there were no more petals, she told her husband and children:

–Come, supper is ready.

A moment later she starved to death.

The Mexican woman had already gathered a little more than a franc to spend the 14th. All together they went out into the street, so that the children could stroll. What joy! What splendor!

The little boys, weak and sick, as they passed in front of the sideboards, said:

–Mom, what's in heaven? Roast chicken?

–And ham? –And cakes?

The oldest girl, the fourteen-year-old, looked sadly at the shop windows of the fashion stores. She was beautiful, and she was leaving without the world having known her! Maybe the poor thing didn't believe in heaven, but in the hospitable death she did. The music of the wind did not deceive her ears; the fireworks did not deceive her eyes; the promises of heaven did not deceive her imagination. Yes, the rocket rises; it also shines, it wants to reach the stars... but it is extinguished in the air. What is certain is the frame, it is the skeleton of the "castle" that shone a moment. And what is certain is the night, densely black.

She was the first to say:

–Shall we go now?

And the younger children, in chorus, repeated:

–Yes, daddy, let's go to heaven.

They bought bread on the way. They were hungrier, much hungrier. They devoured that bread in their room. The father didn't; he couldn't. The mother didn't; she didn't want to.

But every penny had been used in that bread. And to sleep well, to sleep as they wanted, coal was indispensable.

–Ah, there's no care! –said the elder. The concierge trusts me.

And she went out. And she brought it.

There was no need for them to extinguish the candle. It also went out. The coal burned, and its Dantean glow resembled a gap from hell in the shade. Who weeps? Who sobs? Who suffocates blasphemies? Who drowns?

Suffocation first takes the little child by the breast; then it gags the weakest; it binds the parents so that they may witness, impotent, the agony of their children; and in the midst of this horror and this frightful silent struggle, the voice of the eldest daughter tears the silence:

–No more! I don't want to die anymore! Father, forgive me!

***

The next day a neighbor broke the door: inside were the corpses. They took them out into the air, made unheard of efforts... All useless!

Wasn't that scene horrible? Life invented a punishment, invented a torture that Dante had not dreamed of. The mother was alive!

Ah, this one exceeds all torments! Ugolino devours his children; but he carries them within himself. And Ugolino dies. Death did not want that mother.

***

Where is he? Hasn't God appeased himself? Hasn't he let her die? Good heavens! When I attend the festivities of this day, when I see so many well-dressed children laughing and playing in the kermesse, I think of the innocent creatures who, hungry and asphyxiated, perished two years ago, and I say to good souls:

–A charity, for God's sake!

...Lord, where is the poor Mexican woman? If she is still alive, give her death as alms!

The white dress

May, the bouquet of wet lilacs that Spring clings to its bodice; May, that of the lukewarm, indecisive dreams of puberty; May, the silver clarion, that plays reveille to the lazy poets; May, that overflows so many flowers as the boats of Myssira: your clear eyes close in voluptuous ecstasy and the promising "until tomorrow" escapes from your lips like a blue butterfly among the petals of a lily.

Not long ago I came out of the chapel, all covered with white roses, and entertained me in seeing the noisy hubbub of the girls who, with white suits, candid veils and orange blossom buttons on their headdress, had gone to offer fragrant bouquets to Mary. May and Mary are two names that are twinned, that soften the word; two smiles that recognize each other and love each other. I don't know what thread of the Virgin unites the two. One is like the echo of the other. May is the pommel and Mary is the essence.

The rich girls got jovially into their carriages; the nannies wore gala clothes; holy pride expressed in their eyes, still weeping, their mothers. They had just received the confirmation of motherhood.

In one of those groups I distinguished my friend Adrian; I went out to meet him; I kissed the little girl, who still does not know how to talk but with her parents and with her dolls; I felt that fresh smell of innocence, of duvet, of maternal arms, that spread the healthy, beautiful and happy creatures; And when the little dove with shy, closed wings left with the mother and the governess, the girl blushing and really, for the first time, Adrian and I, tireless walkers, moved away from the streets filled with people on Sundays, to go to the road that shades the trees and that lovers look for at dusk and the friends of solitude at noon.

Adrian is a mystic; but he is not, strictly speaking, a believer. A lamp stolen from the sanctuary, its flame oscillates, rebellious in the open air; but the oil that feeds it is the same that made it shine, like an ecstatic pupil, when, already sleeping the prayer, it watched over the temple. That flame still seeks the look of the nuns who prayed matins in the low choir; it still feels with delight the cold of dawn, entering through the ogives; is still frightened by the black body of the owl, anxious to sip it.

Like this one, there are many souls in which the beliefs have been transformed into specters, disturbing the sleep with moans, only perceptible to them, or in luminous but mute spirits; sad souls, like an island in the middle of the ocean, looking with envy at the submissive wave and the resolutely rebellious wave; souls whose ideals resemble stalactites of an obscure grotto, under whose vaults the night wind mooes; souls who see themselves living, as if they always had some mirror in front of them, and at times, fearful, apprehensive, or moved by high aesthetic and moral sense, close their eyes not to look at each other; souls from whose deepest hollow always peeks a vigilant and hard judge; souls that not feeling owners of themselves, but slaves of superior and ignored powers, cry out in the shadow. "Where is he, who is my master?".

Adrian, subject to all influences, good and bad; petal in the human whirlpool; susceptible to enthusiasm and faintness, had that morning the spirit in a cloud of incense. He had returned to the age when no one called him "father" and he said: "Father!". But since in him joy projects its inseparable shadow of sadness; as he is always accompanied by "the poor child dressed in black who resembles him as a brother", he spoke to me thus of his recent joy:

–You don't know how much melancholy a white dress produces, when one has already lived a lot for oneself or for others. This morning, when I saw next to my little girl's bed, the immaculate suit that she was going to wear to offer the Virgin beautiful flowers for the first time; when I touched that very subtle veil that seems to melt like fog, if we want to grab it; I felt the vanity of the father whose daughter begins to take the first steps, to babble the first prayers, and who, dressed with pride, happy because she lacks nothing and ignores everything, walks to the temple, now consciously and as a white molecule integral to Christian communion. I kissed her with more kisses inside each one than other times. I smiled, laughed when I saw her looking at herself and admiring herself in the mirror, as if she was asking: "Is that me?". I loved the natural clumsiness with which she used to walk in her little bedroom, taking care that the rub does not affect her dress and raising it with her hand so that it would not touch the carpet. Once in the carriage, we put her in her seat like a little fairy tale princess who is going to marry the blue king. It looked like a living wafer, and it is truly the wafer of my soul.

In the temple, the ceremony is not solemn, it is tender. Solemn, the imposition of priestly orders; solemn, the taking of the habit; solemn, the office of the deceased; solemn, the pomp of Catholic worship in the great days of the Church; tender, lived, pure, this angelic procession of intact souls that brings flowers to the Virgin.

The candles appeared to me as little bodies of children who lost weight, died and were saved; little bodies whose chaste soul shines, in the form of a flame, fixed in the white girls who are going to put the first leaves of their nest on the altar of Mary. The Mother of God seems like more motherly surrounded by all those virginities, ignorant even that they are; by all those innocencies that invoke her. The girls feel as if they have grown up.

They took mine with the smallest ones. They took her without her resisting. They took her... Do you know what that phrase means? Before and recently, I was alone at home... at home, that is, in my domains. From that moment on, she was going with others, without missing me and her mother; she no longer belonged to us as much as the day before; our hands were no longer her only support; her will, huddled together before, would open its wings. From the children's choir rose the stammering song, like a litany of love, heard from afar. I saw her come down with some work from the bench and go step by step, still hesitant, with her bouquet of flowers, to the steps of the altar. And she did not fall, nor did she weep, nor did she return to see us; they caressed her, smiled at her, asked her name, and those smiles prayed to my spirit, like the breath of unknown affection that I shall never find again.

She left; but she left with the Virgin, with the ideal of love, with the ideal of pain clothed with hope. I did leave her with the Virgin Mary without fear, because I was certain that she was going to return her to me, and if not to me, to her mother, because she was a mother. Something like lustral water fell from my being. Yes, turn over, daughter, your basket of white buttons on the steps of the altar; tell the Virgin to put, by candle, an angel's wing in the boat of your life; ask her for purity, which is the holy ignorance of painful pleasure... but what are you going to ask of her if you only know how to ask for toys and the word life does not yet crystallize in your understanding nor, inquiring, has it come out of your lips?

Then, I saw her coming back. The orange blossoms trembled in her blond curls: she looked like a bride. She was holding in her hand another girl, shorter in stature: she looked like a mother.

These two words: girlfriend... mom... said inwardly, woke up in the deep echoes of my spirit I do not know what terrifying rumors. There is another white dress, such as this one of offering flowers, perhaps more luxurious, richer in clouds of lace; dress of resonant and long cauda. There are other orange blossoms that do not jump joyfully in the mobile heads of the girls, but they are still and rigid in the hair of the betrothed. That dress will wait in the couch, when the sad morning of tomorrow arrives.

Now, that white dress, those orange blossoms, I gave them to her; they are mine, because she is mine. But... the other, the others, will be from someone I don't know, from someone who will come, with more power than I, to tear her from me, because humanity is perpetuated by the inescapable law of ingratitude. And then, that boat will not return to the shore where I am, after a brief crossing in the still lake; it will be lost in the high sea of life, without me being able to protect it; without it being possible for me to swim and reach it. How, in what tone, will the word LIFE then spring from those lips? In that sea the mist emerges; there the Unknown human says out loud his innermost secret; there only when the exasperated pain cries out, the father hears... the poor father who, from afar, guesses and keeps silent.

When you feel this moral anguish, turn your spirit to the Virgin, saying: "Open your eyes so that there will be light. She brings you flowers: as you have so many, keep the ones she offers you for her". And I don't know if because the light of candles inflames our eyes, we shed some tears that the heat or the male pride evaporate.

Isn't the white dress suggestive? To be a bride... to be a mother... to truly ask the Virgin... to know what life is... The white suit is already dressed in mourning!

And there is another white suit... Oh, no, never; there is no other white suit!

***

My friend, the mystic, like Verlaine and like Rod, had taken the last sip of the green opal that gives sleep and death.

Chronicle of a thousand colors

I

Once upon a time there was a young girl in a village, so pretty that it was a pleasure to see her! The beauty of the girl drove her mother and grandmother crazy; the grandmother was the housekeeper in the castle of Saint-Loup.

The girl was no more or less simple than her companions; what happened was that since a trip she made to Paris with her grandmother, she had taken so much advantage that, imitating the "chic" of the Parisians, she passed as the funniest and most interesting girl of her village.

What happened in this trip to the capital of the civilized world?

Nothing worth mentioning. The grandmother had undertaken it to collect a legacy of a few hundred silver coins, which dissipated like smoke in the purchase of sweets and ornaments for the use of the granddaughter, who had wanted to rehearse her small teeth in the great art of swallowing inheritances.

II

At the age of thirteen, our heroine was no longer a child; her waist was fine and well-formed, her breast was white, her eyes big and black, and her hands small and white.

She was flirtatious,
Malicious,
Provocative,
Wilful,
Vain,
Gluttonous,
Capricious,
Inquisitive,
And hypocritical.

In short, she summed up all the qualities that are necessary for a well-bred young woman.

In the summer, in order to avoid the air that slits the skin, and the sun that burns it, she had the habit of using a small shawl, of wool.

In winter she used the same shawl, understanding with her nascent flirtatiousness that it looked very good on her.

To the custom of using that a little extravagant headdress owed the nickname with which she was known, rather than to its similarity with the Little Purple Hood, that the evil wolf found so confident, as tender and succulent.

III

One day, his mother, who had baked cookies, said to her:

"Go to the castle to see how your grandmother is, for I have been assured that she is ill, and give her this cookie and this little jar of butter from me".

The young girl, who did not wish, nor had any other illusion than to run through the fields and plantations, took the little jar of butter in her right hand, put the cookie under her left arm, and threw herself into the light field like a butterfly rehearsing its nascent wings.

She was fifteen years old, a happy age when the soul gives itself to love as the flower gives itself to the rays of the sun, although she did not know how to conjugate the verb love as the grammars teach us.

But on the other hand she had in her fingers, without having learned it, the complicated art of double bookkeeping, according to ancient and modern methods.

Debit and Credit had no hidden difficulties for her.

Capital!
Interest!
In the till!

Were the only words contained in her dictionary.

In the meantime, her little companions said: I love you! to everything that breathes, the bird that passes by and the lover that stops; but she said: If, as I hope, at the age of twenty I have put one million in the till, the capitalized interests will soon give me two; and when I have three, I think that still I'll be young.

See the secret of this anomaly:

The good fairies who presided over the birth of our heroine, had taken the height of her favors to the point of depriving her of that organ of luxury, which is called heart and which is the primitive cause of all human ills and sorrows.

IV

In one of his raids, Little Pink Riding Hood, found the only son of the old Baron of Saint-Loup, one morning, accompanied by his preceptor.

The glances of both young people meet like a double artillery fire.

The young woman did not look down at this meeting. On the contrary, she stared at the gentleman Avenant de Saint-Loup and smiled at him, showing off her beautiful teeth:

"Good morning, Monsignor!".

The young man blushed as the young girl should have done, and stammered:

"Good morning, miss", barely noticeable.

The gentleman Avenant was twenty years old, had a nice figure, blue eyes like the blue of the sky and blond hair like those of Apollo; but his intelligence did not correspond to the qualities mentioned before; he was a bit of a simpleton not to say a harsher word about such a kind gentleman.

–Here is a handsome young man, told herself the Little Pink Riding Hood after the first meeting. Soon I will swallow him and make him love me to the point of delirium, or rather I will make him marry me, which is the same thing.

I already have him here and here, she added, touching her forehead and the place where others have their hearts; the day will come when I will become the wife of my lord's son.

In spite of the revolution that clumsily believes to have abolished forever the titles and lordships, the man who inhabits the castle or the best country house of a village, is always the lord in the eyes of the countrymen, who would think themselves dishonored if they could not give this name to someone, even if this someone was a rascal, enriched in the prison or a retired apothecary.

V

Two mountains do not meet, says the wisdom of nations, but two young people do meet, especially when they have no other desire than to meet.

The Little Pink Riding Hood continued meeting Avenant on the road, several times; by chance, something planned and arranged beforehand.

The young man still blushed, but blushed less; soon he stopped blushing; he came to articulate almost intelligible words, then very clear phrases. Finally, one day, three times blissful, he dared to take the hand of the village girl and bring her with gallantry to his lips.

From that moment the appointments followed one another without interruption, and the astute young girl, wanting to precipitate the outcome she had dreamed of, prepared her net with Machiavellianism worthy of the deceased Lovelace, which has never existed.

VI

So she left for the castle with her biscuit and her little jar of butter.

While she considered that her mother could see her, she followed the royal path with a small step, just as a reasonable person must walk on the floor taken care of by the prefect; but at the first bend of the path the course changed abruptly and she ran all the way along a path leading directly to the park of the castle of Saint-Loup, where she was sure to find the gentlemanly Avenant. She had barely begun her crazy race, when suddenly she came face to face with the old man from Saint-Loup, who was coming back from hunting.

–Where are you going in such a hurry, beautiful girl? he said to her, holding both her hands.

–I'm going to the castle, Baron, I'm going to deliver this cookie and this little jar of butter to my grandmother, answered the Little Pink Riding Hood, lowering her eyes with great humility and candor.

–If you go to the castle, we'll go together, little one; and incontinently, he tried to kiss her.

–Impossible, said the village girl, saving herself with the lightness of a frightened fawn; I'm not going the same way as the gentleman baron.

–What does it matter, your path will be mine.

–Really? but mine will not be yours; my mother has strongly advised me to avoid the company of men, and especially that of wolves.

–Cruel child, according to that, you don't want to love me.

–That I love you not, lord baron? on the contrary, I esteem you and venerate you.

–Who the hell is asking you for your veneration? exclaimed the angry baron, am I an old man of one hundred and seven years old? Ah! if you would listen to me for a while... nothing more than a while, I would do to please you.

–Really?

–By my honor as a gentleman! Try it immediately.

–Well, take my biscuit and my little jar to the castle. Put it in the office, from where I will take it and I will appreciate it very much.

I'll take them and later I'll tell you how I understand your apprecia-tion. When will I see you again, mischievous girl?

–Probably early tomorrow... because it's late enough, and I'll have to stay in the castle with my grandmother. Goodbye, Baron, and she started to run again.

–If you wanted to, if you wanted to... gentle Little Pink Riding Hood, said the old Baron of Saint-Loup again, running and limping after her.

–Yes, yes, it's good, I know your saying, you've told me that more than once.

–I will love you very much.

The little village girl was still running.

–I will make you rich.

The little village girl kept on running.

–I will make you happy.

The little village girl kept on running.

–I'll make you Baroness of Saint-Loup.

The little village girl suddenly stopped.

"Baroness!", he said Baroness? she asked herself, making herself all ears to hear it again, but uselessly, because the poor lord of Saint-Loup, no longer being able to cope with the race fell rolling on the lawn.

Bah! Bah! she said to herself; well, I am not a fool to be concerned by the statements of this old madman! By marrying her son I will also become a baroness, and my husband will be young, beautiful and foolish, three great qualities for a husband! Go away, go away, you ugly old man, you must not be the one who swallows the little girl; the little girl, on the contrary, will be the one who swallows your little wolf, who is really handsome.

VII

At the end of a quarter of an hour of race the little village girl arrived and sneaked into the park of the castle of Saint-Loup.

–What's the matter? She said to the young Avenant, whom she found sitting on a bench of moss granite, with a sad, dejected countenance, what happened to you, my beautiful gentleman?

–The greatest of misfortunes.

–I understand: you have spoken of our marriage to the Baron and he has refused to give his consent.

–It is the truth.

–I expected it. But it is the same, Avenant you have given a proof of courage; and I am glad of you, in proof of it, come and kiss me on both cheeks as a reward.

The young man obeyed with his eyes low.

Now, sit beside me, and let us speak seriously, but first of all give me your handkerchief, so that I may wipe away the sweat that runs down your forehead. Poor child! you are not yet accustomed to the struggles of life! Look how your beautiful eyes are red. You have cried, and your blond hair is stuck to your temples, as if you had taken a bath. Dear angel, don't tremble like this: am I not near you to defend our happiness? she added, taking a protective tone and putting back on the shawl, which had been removed so that Avenant could kiss her more easily.

–Now go back to the castle, and pack your suitcases.

–What for? Said Avenant, looking at Little Pink Riding Hood with a surprised look.

–What for? Have you not understood, then, innocent child, that as a consequence of your foolish confession the baron will send spies to track you?

–And we shall never see each other again.

–Heavens!

–And if he catches us together, he will lock you up in your room.

–It's very probable!

–And your Little Pink Riding Hood will die of sorrow far from his beloved.

–Jesus Mary!

–I have already found a remedy for our evils, she said laughing out loud. This afternoon I will steal you; that is, you will steal me and we will leave for Paris; there we will find money in the pockets of the moneylenders, of people of whom we will say much evil after they have served us; I know perfectly well how all this is done. You will sign documents with imaginary dates, payable annually. Come on, frightened boy, console yourself and smile at me, let me see your pretty teeth whiter than the milk of my beautiful black cow.

–But how shall I pay in a year's time?

–Is it necessary to tell you? Won't you be of age within six months?

–Yes.

Well, you will sell your crops.

–They're from my dad...

–Your beautiful farms.

–They also belong to my father.

–Your beautiful woods.

–They also belong to Dad.

–Your great castle.

–It belongs to Dad.

–According to that, it's all your father's, said the Little Pink Riding Hood, standing up suddenly.

–Yes, my mother was poor, all our fortune belongs to our father, but my teeth, my hair, my eyes and my smile that you love so much belong to me.

–This was all I needed, reflected the young woman, my business failed.

–But rest assured, said Avenant, who, in spite of everything and his innocence, had noticed the distress of his beloved; I have found an infallible means to reconcile everything, and in the end my father will grant us what I want.

–Let us see your plan, said the little girl, believing for a moment that Avenant was less of an imbecile than she had imagined.

–We will leave together and immediately as you wish: we will love each other tenderly and we will work so that we can sustain ourselves. We will marry when the law permits, and when we have half a dozen children, they will throw themselves at the feet of their grandfather, who will forgive us, as soon as he knows how much we have suffered.

–Is that your project? And do you think, sir, that I am a girl capable of diverting a young man from his duties? you are mistaken, good-bye –and she turned his back on poor Avenant, who was left dazed and stunned with such an unexpected escape.

And the Little Pink Riding Hood said: The baron is old and ugly, but rich and adores me. Well... instead of the wolf cub, I will swallow the old wolf. It's harder, it's true, but at least I have good teeth.

The young woman hastened her steps, for the night was already beginning to shade the earth; one could only distinguish one light from another in the castle, and the large poplars moved by the wind seemed to greet the future owner of the domain as they passed by.

VIII

After lifting his seventy-two-year-old body from the ground, the baron said:

"For the coat of arms of my parents, cross my heart and hope to die if I am not madly in love with that delicious Little Pink Riding Hood, like a common villain, and I will not leave it to the my naive son who is not yet old enough to be able to appreciate such a tasty snack. It doesn't matter! I have some Richelieu in my right eye and some Lauzun in my left nose, won't I succeed with a little village girl? We will see that, by the blue blood that circulates in my veins! The revolutions will have been able to abolish the privileges; but not to weaken my race! I am what my grandparents were;

I am worth what my ancestors were. My great-great-grandfather 'messiere le Loup' swallowed the Little Purple Riding Hood. I will swallow mine. My great-great-grandfather's Little Riding Hood was purple, mine will be pink; at last the color doesn't matter at all. It's about playing a trick, a 'regency' style trick".

And the baron began to dig up the memories of his youth.

"By my honor", said to himself, after mature reflection "that old tricks are always the best, for the simple reason that they have already served many times. Tonight it will enter in my housekeeper's room, I will drive away the old woman with any pretext, and when the Little Pink Riding Hood arrives, we will see!".

IX

While the old baron was absorbed in his amatory ideas, the Little Pink Riding Hood returned to the castle, fast as only can be a fifteen years old girl, and knocked on his grandmother's door.

...Knock, knock!...

–Who is it?

–I am your granddaughter.

The good grandmother who was lying down because she was sick shouted from her bed:

–Pull the string of the lock and the door will open.

The young woman pulled the string and the door opened.

As she entered, she threw herself into her grandmother's arms, ate her with kisses, and told her I don't know what story.

The only thing I can say is that the old woman hurriedly dressed, and followed her granddaughter without hesitation behind the courtyard, where she was locked up with three turns of the key, by the cruel girl, without pity for her venerable age, nor respect for her sacred title of grandmother.

If I haven't forgotten the story of the Little Purple Riding Hood from whom I descend directly, was reflecting the little village girl as she reached her grandmother's room, which was also a dining room and living room, the wolf will come to try to deceive the old lady, and everything will be arranged. Will it upset her?

–I don't think so.

–In the meantime, let's set the table; the conversation is best enjoyed over dinner.

She had barely put the tablecloth on an old, lame table when somebody knocked on the door.

Knock, knock!

–Who is it?

The Baron of Saint-Loup, who wanted to enter the place by cunning instead of invoking his rights as lord and master, answered:

–Your granddaughter asked me to give you a biscuit and a small jar of butter sent to you by her mother.

Little Pink Riding Hood replied by thickening her voice:

–Pull the latch cord and the door will open.

The old baron pulled the string and the door opened.

The young woman, upon seeing him enter, threw a long, loud laughter.

–Sit down, Mr. Baron, and let's have supper while my grandmother comes. She went to the neighboring forest to see if the young goats are doing well.

The baron sat down.

And dinner was cheerful.

And the girl did not swallow the wolf, the first night; but fine as amber, she did not allow him to swallow her either.

However, its severity did not reach the degree of despair; she granted him a little, very little, enough to make him want more.

X

The next day, the old baron installed the Little Pink Riding Hood in a beautiful house located two arquebus shots from the castle, where she lived as a "Thousand and One Nights" princess.

The farms, the woods and the unemployed have already been swallowed; the barony has not yet been swallowed, but it will be achieved, by means of this slow and sure step that is known to no one but the woman and the turtle.

The baron caresses her from the hand to the elbow, but when it happens that he wants to pass from that point; she repels him with the tip of her fan, telling him with a graceful smile:

–I wish to be Baroness of Saint-Loup!

Twenty times an hour and a hundred times a day, the baron hears these eternal words resounding in her ear, like a funereal touch.

–I wish to be Baroness of Saint-Loup!

At last comes the day when more in love and repelled than ever the baron falls at her feet and exclaims:

–In eight days you will be Baroness of Saint-Loup.

XI

The most skillful seamstresses of Paris were called to fix the dresses of the miss who will soon be a lady.

The whole town is on the move.

Only the gentleman Avenant is missing from the party.

The cunning little village girl, judging that one day or another, this young man could serve as an obstacle to her ambition, has managed to convince his father to send him to travel the world and complete his education. At this time he is in Palestine, the place where his grandparents covered themselves with glory, back in the year 1160.

XII

On the day appointed for these happy weddings, at dawn, the future baroness, already dressed, with corset and gloves, is ready for the ceremony and sends to warn the Mayor and the Priest.

At noon they come to announce to her that everyone is ready and that only the bridegroom is missing.

She runs to the baron's room, knocks and nobody answers. She enters... nothing. – She calls him... nothing... she runs deader than alive, towards the baron's bed, she draws the curtains violently... and sees! Wow, she mutters softly without even blinking; this is what I call swimming, swimming and drowning on the shore, happily I can yet swallow up the little boy! And incontinent, in the same room of the deceased, she writes the following letter:

"My dear Avenant:

"Come, your dear father is dead, and your Little Pink Riding Hood, who loves you tenderly, is waiting for you to lead you to the altar.

XIII

Avenant returns using post-horses; he arrives with big, gummed mustaches, stronger than when he left for Palestine, but not even with half the cunning of a sixteen-year-old girl.

–Dear Avenant, she says to him when she sees him, throwing herself around his neck, how I have wept for you! but now that you are here, let us forget everything.

–Little Pink Riding Hood, how sweet of you!

–It's to please you, my beautiful.

–What beautiful arms your have!

–It's to hold you better.

–How big are your eyes!

–It's to see you better, my darling.

–How white and small are your teeth!

–It's to bite you better, my beautiful.

And so much so that she bit him with such good manners that she finally became Baroness of Saint-Loup.

Conclusion

The author from whom I took this legend concludes the story by saying:

If you have not mocked my story, dear and honest readers, you must agree with me that the times, the young women and the men have changed a lot! Today it is no longer the wolf who swallows the small girl; it is the small girl who swallows the wolf.

History of a counterfeit peso

He looked good! Clean, very brushed, with his eagle, like a tie pin, and always walking on the side of the shadow, to leave the other sidewalk in the sun! He didn't have a bad face and the one who only knew him by sight wouldn't have hesitated to trust him with four pesetas. But... Don't believe in the white gray hairs and in the silver that shines! That peso[1] was a dyed peso: his hair was brown, made of copper, and he was coquettish, because he liked to be told: "you are very Louis XVI", he had dusted it.

Of course it was from unknown parents. These poor little pesos are always foundlings! They inspire me a great deal of pity, and I would gladly collect them; but my house, that is, their house, the pocket of my vest, is empty, unfurnished, full of air, and so I cannot receive them. When some of them falls on me, I try to place him in a canteen, in a shop, in the accounting office of the theater; but today there placements are very expensive and the poor peso almost always stays in the street.

It did not happen the same, however, with that one with a good face, with a good smile and an eagle that seemed truthfully. I do not know where they gave it to me, but I am certain of which is the house of commerce where I had the fortune to place it, thanks to the good heart and to the bad sight of the respectable merchant whose name I keep quiet for not offend-

---

1 Ancient silver coin, used in Spain and its colonies, which had different values, and from where the monetary unit called peso comes from.

ing the Christian annoyance of so excellent subject and for the maxim that says that the left hand must ignore the good that did the right one.

That is, as a benefit is never lost, and as God rewards the charitable, the generous putative father of my false peso did not take long to find another gentleman who would consent to take charge of the creature. Evil tongues say that this philanthropic trait was not altogether pure; it seems that the new protector of my peso (and it must be understood that the merchant to whom I entrusted the upbringing and education of the poor foundling was a bartender) did not realize exactly that he was going to do a work of mercy, because repeated libations had somewhat obscured his sight and hindered his touch. But, either because that man had a noble heart, or because cognac predisposes to benevolence, the fact is that my man received the false peso not with open arms, but by stretching out his right hand. He gave the bartender a five-pesos bill, and got back four pesos from the bartender, and among those four, as a poor friend in the company of the rich, it was my peso.

But see how the poor are good and how God has adorned us with the virtue of dogs: fidelity! The four capitalists, the four silver pesos, the aristocrats, went on a rampage. There is no doubt that the aristocracy is very corrupt! One stayed in a tavern, other in the Concordia, and the other one in the ticket office of the theater... Only the false peso, the poor man, the middle class, the one who was neither a penny nor a decent person, continued to accompany his generous protector as Cordelia accompanied King Lear! It was at Concordia where they met him; there they threw his poverty in his face and did not want to trust him or serve him anything. The last good coin then escaped with the boy (it is not new that a well-born young lady escapes with a kitchen hand), and there remained the poor peso, the one that did not have anything, but a heart that was not yet metallized, accompanying the helper in his orphanage, in sadness, in abandonment, in misery? The same as Cordelia next to King Lear!

These counterfeit pesos are really touching! While the so-called good ones, those of high ancestry, those born in the opulent National Mint, lead a bad life and go from hand to hand like the venal journalists, like the defecting politicians, like the coquettish women; while these impenitent vicious ones spend the night in the inn, buy the virtue of the maidens and spurn the needy to go with the rich; the counterfeit peso looks for the poor and does not abandon him, in spite of the bad treatment he always gives him; he does not go out; he is locked up in his house; he does not buy anything, and waits, as only a reward for such exalted virtues, for martyrdom; the ingratitude of man; to be apprehended, after all, by the gendarme without entrails or to die nailed to the wood of a counter, as San Dimas died on the cross. Poor counterfeit pesos! They break my soul when I see them in the hands of others.

The one in my story, however, had begun his life well. God protected him for being handsome, yes, for being good, in spite of the fact that the skeptical waiter of Concordia did not believe in such goodness, for being simple, for being innocent, for being honest. He didn't steal anything from me; neither from the bartender; and from the gentleman who took him out of the canteen, where he wasn't at ease, because fake pesos are very sober, he rewarded the good work by giving him a beautiful illusion: the illusion that he still had a peso.

And he didn't just do that... You'll see what he did!

The gentleman remained in the inn, meditative and sad, before the cup of tea, the glass of Bordeaux, now without Bordeaux, and the waiter standing in front of him as a question mark. That situation could not be prolonged. When someone is alone with an innocent counterfeit coin, he is ashamed as if he were with a lost woman; he wants them not to see him, to spend incognito, that no friend surprises him? Because counterfeit coins will be very good... but people don't want to believe it!

I myself, in the first lines of this story, when I had not yet found a putative father for the fake peso, called him a rogue. So imperious is the power of the vulgar!

Still the gentleman, in a moment of bad mood that I don't excuse in him, but that I would have excused in me, after they removed the table-cloths from the table, hit the peso against the marble, as if to say to him: "Well, evil, if you really don't have a heart!" –And he had a heart! What the unhappy man didn't have was money.

The gentleman was meditative for a long time. Who had given him that peso? Remembrances were still in his memory, as indecisive, as distracted, as sleepy. But there was no doubt: the peso was fake! And what's worse, it was the last one!

Its owner then began to make, not for his own use, a whole moral treatise.

The truth is –he said to himself– that I am a fool. This afternoon at the office I received a twenty-fifty note. I seem to be seeing it... London-Mexico... the eagle... Don Benito Juarez... and... Where's the banknote?

> In the bushes of life he leaves
> One thing each: the sheep
> His white wool; man his virtue!

And the bad thing is that my wife was waiting for those twenty. I was going to give her fifteen... but where do I get those fifteen now?.

The gentleman threw the counterfeit peso back on the marble table in anger. The unfortunate eagle, the tie pin, almost broke! The only advantage of fake pesos is that we can't crash them into a corner.

To the street! The Emerald, who no longer dances on the oriental tapestry nor gracefully touches her tambourine; the poor Emerald, who is now employed in the corner of Plateros and who, like the ancient night watchmen, gives the hours, showed our hero her luminous watch: it was twelve o'clock at night.

At such a time, there's no money on the street. And I had to go home!

–I'll give my wife the fake peso for breakfast, and tomorrow... We'll see! But no! She rings them on the desk and I'm sure I won't escape an argument. Damn luck...!

The poor peso suffered in silence the insults and scratches of his putative father, hidden in the darkest part of his pocket. Alone, sadly alone!

The gentleman passed in front of a gambling house. Would he come in? Maybe some friend was in it. Besides, they knew him there... they even collected from time to time his fortnights... At least, they could extend him credit for five silver dollars... He looked back and came inside fast as who rushes into the pool.

The cashier friend was not on duty that night; but he would probably come back at one o'clock. The gentleman stood by the roulette table. I don't know what charm that little ivory ball that runs, jumps, laughs and gives or takes money has; but it's so little, it's so cute! It looks like Luisa Théo! The pesos, arranged in columns were ready for the battle, formed in the boxes of the green carpet. And our man was certain that the next number was going to be the 32! He had seen it! Would he bet the fake peso...? The truth is that it was not very correct... But, after all, in that house they knew him... and... How they would suspect!

With his somewhat trembling hand, he opened his wallet as if looking for a bank note (which, of course, was not at home), closed it again, removed the peso, and resolutely, with the gesture of a great lord, put it at the 32. His heart was jumping more than the ivory ball in the roulette. But you see how things are! Good young men have a long way to go... There are men who come to be foreign ministers, rich men, poets, wise men, just because they are good young men. And that peso –he had already said it– was a good-looking young man... a good-dressed young man.

–Thirty-two red!

The ivory ball and the player's heart stopped, like the clock whose wheel breaks. He had won! But... What if they knew him...? Not him... the other... the fake one!

Our friend (because he must already be our friend, this pampered son of bliss) had a genius trait. He picked up his peso scornfully and said to the roulette man:

–I want the other thirty-five on paper.

They hadn't touched it! They hadn't met him...! The house paid him. One of twenty... one of ten... and another, color of chocolate, with the figure of a woman in a nightgown, resting from reading, separated by these two words "Five pesos", from the portrait of a very pretty girl, whom the bad taste of the engraver had an eagle and a snake placed on her chest. The ten one and the one the color of chocolate were for the lady who rings the pesos on the lid of the desk. The twenty, the Juarez, the patriotic, was for our friend... it was the one that the next day would turn into cups, into a Milanese rib and, at the end, into a sad and desolate fake peso.

How fortunate are counterfeit pesos and rogue men!

Those around the green mat were making space to the blissful player so that he would enter the table and sit down. But, to honor our good friend, he was prudent, had strength of spirit, and turned his back to the treacherous table. He would return, yes, he would leave in it his future fortnight, or, properly speaking, the simple future of his fortnight; but in that night he was given over to the delights and pinches at home.

When he was in the street with his honest, generous fake peso, which had been so good; and with the portrait of Juarez, with the bust of a dog, and with the engraving that represents a lady in a nightgown, our dear friend overflowed with joy. That honest and intelligent gentleman was already as good as the fake peso. He would have lent a penny to any poor friend; he would have distributed some coins among the beggars; walking quickly, quickly through the streets, he thought of his poor wife, who is such a good person and who would be waiting for him... to receive the money.

> *Then, the fickle husband*
> *Returning to the home*
> *To appear wise*
> *Takes on the look of coups,*
> *He thinks about his wife*
> *–Only in his bed–*
> *And from the lady's house*
> *A lover is running away...!*
> *This is the red dawn,*
> *Etc.*

They sing that in an operetta that premiered in Paris at the end of last month called *The Red Egg*, but it wasn't even hummed by our favorite friend because he didn't know it.

Turning a corner, he stumbled upon a certain little boy who was shouting newspapers and who was called "the English". And he looked like an Englishman, really, because he was very white, very blond, and he would have been pretty if he hadn't been so poor. Of course, he didn't know his father..., he was one of so many fake human pesos, those that circulate surreptitiously around the world and that no one knows where they were minted. But he knew his mother! The others said it was bad. He thought it was good. That would be his way of caressing! Also, when you don't eat, it's impossible to be in a good mood. And many times that wretch didn't eat. Above all it was the mother; what you only have once; which always lives not long; the mother who, although bad, is good at times, the one in whose mouth the "you" does not sound like an insult... The mother, in short... nothing more than the mother! And since that boy had good blood in his veins –blood colored with wine, blood impoverished in the nights of orgy, but blood, at last, of men who thought and felt many years ago– he loved his mother very much... and his little sister, whom he sold tickets... that one they called "Frenchy".

The mother, for him, was very good; but she hit him, when the poor boy couldn't bring her a peso. And that night –the night of the fake peso– the little boy was with *The National*, with *Tomorrow's Time*, but without a penny in the pocket of his torn trousers. People didn't buy newspapers! And he did not dare to return to his home, not for fear of the blows but for not afflicting his mother.

So pale, so sad was he seen by the lucky gambler, who wanted, really wanted, to give him alms. Maybe he would have bought him all the newspapers, because that's how gamblers are when they win. But to give five pesos to such a rascal was too much. And the gambler had received the thirty-five in bills. All he had left was the counterfeit peso.

Then a mischief occurred to him: to make a fool of the boy.

–Here, English, for your pages with Catalán, go! Get drunk!

And there was the fake peso!

And no, the boy did not believe that he had been deceived. That gentleman had as good a face as the counterfeit peso. How good he was! If he had received that coin to return seven and a half reals[2], as payment for *The National* or *Tomorrow's Time,* he would have sounded it in the slabs of the hall, whose threshold served him almost as a bed, he would have asked if it was good or not to the grocer who still had his shop open. But as alms! It was so bright at night! It was so bright for his soul, hungry to give something to his mother and little sister! What a good gentleman...! He would have won a prize in the lottery!... He would be very rich! Who knows... What a good lord was the one of the fake peso!

He had told him: "Go, go and get drunk!"... But that's what they all say!

He picked up the newspapers, and, running as if he had eaten, as if he had strength, he went very far, to the door of his house. They didn't open it. The old lady (I call her old lady, even if she beat that boy, because, after all, she was unhappy, she was a father, she was a mother) had fallen asleep tired of waiting for the Englishman. But what did he care about sleeping in

---

2 The real was a silver coin.

the street? If the same thing happened many nights! And the next day he wouldn't be whipped...! He arrived rich... with a peso!

Oh, how many, how many things there are in a peso for the poor!

There, in the hallway, shrunken like a white kitten, the boy fell asleep. Sleeping, yes, but squeezing with the fingers of the right hand, which is the safest, that sun, that eagle, that dream! He slept badly, not because of the hardness of the stone mattress, not because of the cold, not because of the air, because he was used to it, but because he was very happy and very afraid that the silver bird would fly away. Do you think that this boy had never had a peso of his own? Well, there are plenty of them. Besides, the little Englishman wanted to daydream, to speak aloud with his illusions.

First, breakfast... Well, a real one for the three of us! But the pesos have a lot of cents, and the Englishman had long wanted to have a tamale with his chocolate drink. Well: a real and a tlaco[3]. There was a lot of money left... Although he had very strong temptations to show it, to pass it, to sound it, as if it were a rattle, to the little sister, to let the mother see it and think: "I can rest now, because my son supports me". But in seeing it, in taking it, the mother would buy a real tequila. And the boy had a daring project: to spend a real, which was going to be tequila, on a ticket. And, above all, he remembered the rascal who owed some tlacos in the bakery, others in the shop... and it was not impossible for the mother to pay them if he gave her the peso. Less reals!

No! It was more urgent to buy a blanket so that his little sister could make a shirt. The poor girl complained so much about the cold...! Decidedly, to the mother four reals, one tostón[4]... and the other four reals for him, that is, for the tamale, for the ticket, for the blanket... And who knows how many more things! It might even be enough to go to the circus!

What if I won $300 in the lottery with that real one? Three hundred pesos! They must never end! That would have the man who gave him the peso.

***

The light came, that is, it was about to arrive, when the boy stood up. They were sweeping the street... Some donkeys passed by with the tin cans, in which the milk comes from the nearby haciendas. Then the cows passed by... In Santa Teresa they called mass... "Jelly," shouted a harsh voice.

The boy didn't want to enter his house yet. He needed to change his peso. He would arrive late, at six o'clock, at seven o'clock; but with a tostón for the mother, with a blanket, with a sponge cake for the French girl and with a tamale in his stomach. He was going to wait for a certain shop to open, in which they sold everything that was most beautiful, everything

---

3 1/8 of real.

4 50 cent Mexican coin.

that was most useful, everything that was most appealing to him: candles, linen or cotton fabric, clay saints, silk hanks, rockets, tin soldiers, candy, bread, stamps, puppets... How much was needed to live. And precisely at the door sat a woman behind a pot of tamales.

He walked step by step, because it was still very early. It had already become clear. He passed through San Juan of Letrán. From the horse boarding house came a beautiful mare with a yellow leather saddle, taken from the bridle by her owner's boy, probably a German. In front of the Monitor's printing press and almost lying on the pavement tiles, men and children folded the still wet newspapers. Many of these boys were friends of his, and the first impulse he felt was to go and talk to them, to show them the peso... But what if they took it off? The cripple, above all, the cripple was a bad thing.

So the rascal went on without stopping.

The shop was already open. And the first thing, by the way, was the tamale... and it wasn't one, it was two: at last he was rich! And after the tamales, a sponge cake of flour and egg, a rich roll that tasted glorious. They wanted to charge him in advance; but he showed the peso with majestic dignity.

–Now that I'll buy some fabric, I'll change the peso. And he asked for two yards of fabric; he bought a clay grenadier that was worth a cuartilla[5] and who he had the misfortune of losing at his youngest age, because when he took it, with his hand convulsed with emotion, it fell to the ground; They wrapped his fabric in a stripe paper, and he proudly, with the gesture of a sovereign, threw through the air the clean peso, which, falling into the zinc of the counter, gave a cry of frankness, one of those cries that escape in the melodramas to the traitor, the murderer, the real delinquent. The Spaniard had heard, and caught the little boy by the throat.

–Thief! Thief! You're going to pay me!

***

What happened? What happened? The broken grenadier, torn to pieces, on the floor... the Indian screaming... the Spaniard squeezing the poor boy... the mother, the little sister, the French girl far away... further still the illusions... and the gendarme very close!

A police station... a wounded... a drunk... people who saw his bad face... men who accused him of stealing handkerchiefs; he wiped his tears with his shirt! And then Corrections... the hunchback who taught him to do bad things... and outside the mother, who died in the hospital, of alcoholic diarrhea... and the little sister, the French one, to whom, because she didn't sell many tickets, they bought her, and, little by little, the poor thing died.

---

5 Mexican silver coin, worth three cents and an eighth.

Sir! You who turned the water into wine, you who made the thief Dimas a saint, why didn't you deign to turn the fake peso of that child into a good one? Why was it a good peso in the hands of the gambler, and a crime in the hands of the helpless? You are not like hope, like love, like life, fake peso. You are good. Your name is charity. You who blinded Saul on the road to Damascus, why didn't you blind the Spaniard in that store?